The Guernseyman

Historical Fiction Published by McBooks Press

BY ALEXANDER KENT
Midshipman Bolitho
Stand into Danger
In Gallant Company
Sloop of War
To Glory We Steer
Command a King's Ship
Passage to Mutiny
With All Despatch
Form Line of Battle!
Enemy in Sight!
The Flag Captain
Signal—Close Action!
The Inshore Squadron
A Tradition of Victory
Success to the Brave
Colours Aloft!
Honour this Day
The Only Victor
Beyond the Reef
The Darkening Sea
For My Country's Freedom
Cross of St George
Sword of Honour
Second to None
Relentless Pursuit

BY R.F. DELDERFIELD
Too Few for Drums
Seven Men of Gascony

BY DAVID DONACHIE
The Devil's Own Luck
The Dying Trade

BY C. NORTHCOTE PARKINSON
The Guernseyman
Devil to Pay

BY V.A. STUART
Victors and Lords
The Sepoy Mutiny

BY CAPTAIN FREDERICK MARRYAT
Frank Mildmay OR
  The Naval Officer
The King's Own
Mr Midshipman Easy
Newton Forster OR
  The Merchant Service
Snarleyyow OR
  The Dog Fiend
The Privateersman
The Phantom Ship

BY DUDLEY POPE
Ramage
Ramage & The Drumbeat
Ramage & The Freebooters
Governor Ramage R.N.
Ramage's Prize
Ramage & The Guillotine
Ramage's Diamond
Ramage's Mutiny
Ramage & The Rebels
The Ramage Touch
Ramage's Signal
Ramage & The Renegades

BY JAN NEEDLE
A Fine Boy for Killing
The Wicked Trade

BY W. CLARK RUSSELL
Wreck of the Grosvenor
Yarn of Old Harbour Town

BY RAFAEL SABATINI
Captain Blood

BY MICHAEL SCOTT
Tom Cringle's Log

BY A.D. HOWDEN SMITH
Porto Bello Gold

BY NICHOLAS NICASTRO
The Eighteenth Captain

The
Guernseyman

C. Northcote Parkinson

RICHARD DELANCEY NOVELS, NO. 1

McBooks Press
ITHACA, NEW YORK

Published by McBooks Press 2001
Copyright © 1982 by C. Northcote Parkinson
First published in the United States by Houghton Mifflin Co., 1973
First published in the United Kingdom by John Murray Ltd, 1982

Cover painting: *A Naval Engagement* by Philip James Loutherbourgy.
Courtesty of Spink & Son Ltd., London, UK/Bridgeman Art Library.

Library of Congress Cataloging-in-Publication Data

Parkinson, C. Northcote (Cyril Northcote), 1909–
  Guernseyman / by C. Northcote Parkinson.
    p. cm. — (Richard Delancy novels ; no. 1)
  ISBN 1-59013-001-4 (alk. paper)
    1. Delancy, Richard (Fictitious character)—Fiction. 2. Great Britain
  —History, Naval—19th century—Fiction. 2. Napoleonic Wars,
  1800–1815 —Fiction 4. Guernsey (Channel Islands)—Fiction.
  PR6066.A6955 G8 2001
  823'.914—dc21   2001026668

Distributed to the book trade by
LPC Group, 1436 West Randolph, Chicago, IL 60607
800-626-4330.

Additional copies of this book may be ordered from any
bookstore or directly from McBooks Press, 120 West State Street,
Ithaca, NY 14850. Please include $3.50 postage and handling with
mail orders. New York State residents must add sales tax.
All McBooks Press publications can also be ordered by calling
toll-free 1-888-BOOKS11 (1-888-266-5711).
Please call to request a free catalog.

Visit the McBooks Press website at www.mcbooks.com.

Printed in the United States of America

9 8 7 6 5 4 3 2 1

FOR JEREMY

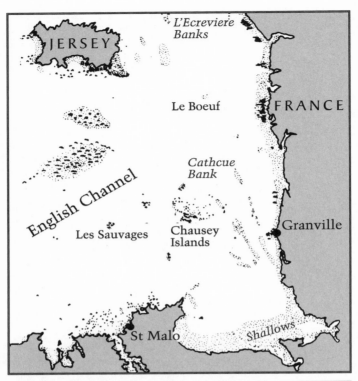

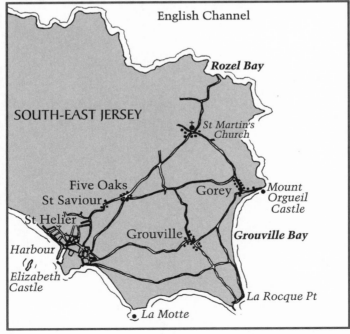

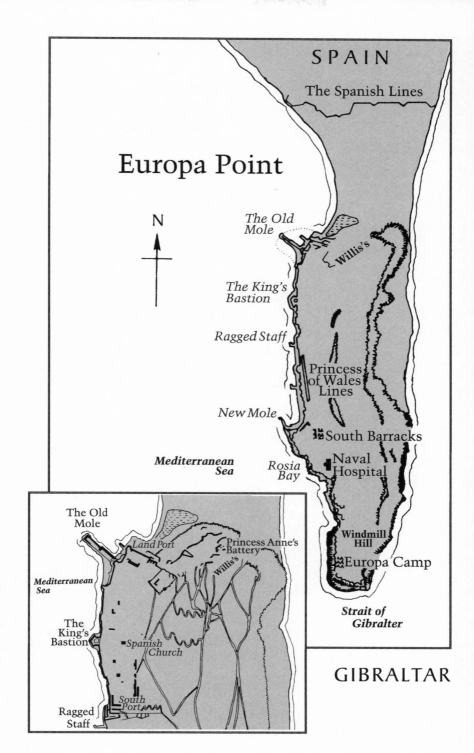

Chapter One

THE GUERNSEYMAN

THE SQUALL came out of the darkness without warning, the brig being laid on her beam-ends. Seamen clung frantically to anything secure and there came from below, just audible over the other noise, the crash of gear displaced and hurled to leeward. A long minute passed during which it seemed that the vessel was lost, and then, slowly, slowly she began to right herself, her masts rising jerkily skywards. Now began the thunder of the tattered sails, whether taken aback or torn to ribbons, with the wind's shriek over all. In the darkness it was hard to tell what canvas, if any, remained and what other damage had been done, but the master, John Beecher, was on deck in a matter of seconds and bellowing his orders at men who might or might not have remained on board. Beecher tried to put the brig before the wind, chancing what dangerous flats might lie to leeward. Working fast, the mate and boatswain, with the four deck-hands, had more than enough to do, even when joined reluctantly by the cook, the steward and a couple of boys. Both topsails had been blown out of the bolt-ropes but finally it was found possible to steer the ship under a close-reefed mainsail. There were hours of work to do and it would be daybreak before all had been even temporarily set to rights. The initial squall had become a westerly half-gale, gusting to gale force occasionally, and the wind still roared overhead, making a noise through which could just be heard the ominous creaking of the pumps.

It had been a bad moment and danger was still far from remote.

John Beecher was a Liverpool man, reared in the coastal trade, and had known these waters since boyhood. A voyage like this, from St Peter Port to Plymouth, from there to Cardiff, and now back to the Mersey, was ordinarily child's play, the more so in that the *Charlotte* (120 tons) was a newish brig and recently re-rigged. He felt confident of making the Mersey but could have wished for a stronger crew. He had sailed originally with one man short and had then left one of his men sick at Plymouth. There was one steerage passenger on board, a youth from Guernsey, one too frightened and ill, he assumed, to be of any use. However, he now had a craft which answered to the helm and he might presently edge round towards his proper course. He would not try to bend another sail until daybreak which was due in another hour or so. With two men at the pump, freeing the vessel of the water that had gone down the hatchway—she was not leaking, he felt sure—and with the old cook nearly use-less, he could spare only two men to clear up the remaining tangle aloft. The brig was proving difficult to handle, however, and he took the weather wheel himself, leaving Otteridge to assist on the lee side. As the other worries lessened he now became aware, for the first time, of the sound forward of a sail flogging itself to tatters. It could only be the jib, a sail he would need if he was to bring the wind abeam, and he knew all too well that the storm jib had already been split. Should he quit the helm and go forward himself? No, he dared not leave Otteridge alone and the mate, Mr Crosbie, was busy in the main-top. With some part of his mind he planned how to make a makeshift jib, using what remained of the fore-topsail or falling back, even, on a hatch cover. He had no sailmaker, however, and doubted whether it could be done in time. But how was he to hold his course without a headsail of some sort?

The noise of snapping canvas died away abruptly and Beecher concluded, with annoyance, that what remained of the sail had gone overboard. Presently, however, an indistinct figure came out of the darkness and a voice at his elbow could be heard, shouting:

"I've secured the jib, sir."

The voice was not one he recognised so the words must have been spoken by his passenger, the young Guernseyman.

"What did you do?" he bawled.

"Knotted the sheet, sir, and made it fast."

"Well done, lad. Are you a seaman?"

"Yes, sir."

"Will you join the crew?"

"If you'll repay me the passage money."

"What's that?"

"Give me my money back—MONEY BACK!"

"Oh—very well."

"What shall I do now, sir?"

"Relieve one of the men on the pump and send him to me."

The wind abated next morning and Beecher could see that his former passenger was pulling his weight. He was not a man but merely a well-grown boy. He was no seaman, whatever he might say. As against that, he was not quite a landlubber, either. Later that day, with the *Charlotte* on course for the Mersey in fairer weather, Beecher sent for the youngster and thanked him.

"What is your name, son?"

"Richard Delancey, sir."

"Is that a Guernsey name?"

"Not really, sir. It is Huguenot, Protestant French."

"What is your real trade?"

"I am to be clerk in a shipowner's counting-house."

"But you have been at sea?"

"In fishing boats, sir."

"Aye, lad, I thought as much. You're used to boats but not to ships."

"Yes, sir."

"Is your father a seaman?"

"No, sir. He is a corn chandler. My great-uncle in Liverpool is a shipowner, though, and I am to work for him."

"Did you never wish to go to sea?"

"I did, sir, but my two elder brothers were lost at sea and my parents did not want to lose me as well."

"Can't say I blame them."

Beecher had nearly offered to take Richard as an apprentice but he lost interest in him after this, repaying his passage money but seeing to it that he earned his keep. He had, of course, much else to think about, and much to do before he sighted Bidston Hill. He was concerned, less immediately, about the news from the American colonies, where there had been fighting at Lexington in April, news of which had reached Liverpool in June. War seemed inevitable with all the inconveniences and dangers that must result, with the press-gangs active and with privateers at sea. One way and another, the outlook seemed bleak.

More interest was shown in Richard by Mr Crosbie, the mate, who taught him some rudiment of seamanship. Some old seaman's clothes, the gear of a man who had deserted, were found for the boy, and he was eventually complimented by the boatswain on his effort at a long splice. It had to be done again, to be sure, but it could have been worse, considered as a first attempt. Convinced for a moment that he had a natural gift for such things, Richard asked Mr Crosbie whether he would be allowed to stay in the ship. He was soon made to realise that there was no chance of this.

"No, son. Not a hope in hell! Liverpool docks will be crowded with men out of work—real seamen at that, men who have rounded the Cape—and who would have a berth for a landsman or little better? We are undermanned because two of our men went down with the flux but at Liverpool we can take our pick. No, my lad—your place is ashore."

"But why are all those seamen out of work, Mr Crosbie? Are things any better at Bristol or London?"

"It's the American trade—all brought to a standstill. There are hundreds of ships lying idle, rotting at their moorings. Seamen can be had for two a penny."

"But what of the other trades, Mr Crosbie? The slave trade? The West Indies?"

"Look, son, the Atlantic is all one. A Liverpool ship carries trade goods to Africa, slaves from Africa to Virginia, tobacco from Virginia back to Liverpool. Take away the American part and the whole voyage comes to nothing."

"But won't that ruin the Americans, too?"

"To be sure it will. So they put to sea as privateers and make the picture worse!"

Thinking this over, Richard came to the conclusion that his prospects in Liverpool as a clerk were no better than his prospects as a seaman. He doubted whether his great-uncle was the sort of man who would pay a boy to do nothing, not even his godson. But what hope had he of returning to Guernsey? As things were, he could not even work his passage. He was still pondering this prospect when the *Charlotte* came into Plymouth. Going ashore there he saw that reception centres had been formed where men were being urged to join the navy. He asked a bystander whether the press-gangs were out but was told that these were not yet needed. Sailors without work were joining as volunteers. The brig sailed again for Cardiff, where the same recruiting efforts were being made. There was only one business prospering and that was the preparation for war. Was that, he wondered, the business he should enter? Ancestors of his had been soldiers. Should he follow the same trade? But what knowledge he had was of the sea. Perhaps he should serve the king that way and end as a captain, perhaps as an admiral! He knew all too little about the service but he guessed that a man who entered on the lower deck would most likely stay there. He sought the advice of the second mate who expressed his horror. "The navy, my lad? That's a service to keep out of! That's the way to find yourself back on the beach without a leg or short of an arm. It may be all right for officers but it's hell on the lower deck."

"But there are midshipmen, surely, no older than I am and in line for promotion. How do they come to be chosen?"

"Midshipmen! A useless and insolent lot of young lubbers, fit for the nursery but strutting on the quarterdeck! They are chosen by the captain, who takes money for it or chooses to oblige a friend. They come aboard as volunteers, first class, sometimes rated as captain's servant, but all classed as "Young Gentlemen." Their fathers make them an allowance through the captain—their pay being next to nothing. They are rated midshipmen when there is a vacancy. If I joined the navy—never fear, I won't—they'd make me master's mate. If *you* joined, you'd be volunteer second class."

"And how do they enter—the volunteers second class?"

"They are shipped from the workhouse, the orphanage or charity school, never having volunteered or been told even what lies ahead of them. They have the worst life of any, the last to be fed and the first to be beaten."

After this conversation Richard felt more resigned to life in a counting-house. He felt still happier about it when the *Charlotte* came into the Mersey on Monday 28 August. On that sunny morning the port looked most impressive, the docks filled with shipping, the town extensive and the country pleasant on the Cheshire side. The pilot had been picked up off Point Lynas, however, and he brought news which was quickly repeated from man to man. There was trouble in the town because the crew of a ship called the *Derby* had been told that their wages would be reduced from thirty to twenty shillings a month. The seamen countered this by unrigging the ship. When some of them were arrested a large crowd of sailors—some thousands, the pilot said—had attacked the gaol and obtained their release. All business was now at a standstill and the more nervous merchants had fled into the country. As the *Charlotte* came into the Salthouse Dock it became obvious that the local atmosphere was tense. No work was being done, no ship was preparing for sea, no goods were being shipped or landed. There were groups of sailors on the quayside and a crowd of them collected in the Goree Piazzas, listening no doubt to one of their leaders. There was no actual riot in progress but it looked as if there might be trouble by nightfall. Nor was it clear that the *Charlotte*'s men would keep out of it. Once the brig was alongside the quay with sails stowed and topmasts sent down, the men went ashore in a group as soon as they had been paid. "They'll end up in prison as like as not," said the boatswain, shaking his head. "Some men can be taught only with a capstan bar."

Feeling very much alone in the world, Richard left his bundle in the brig, with the second mate's permission, and went ashore that afternoon in the clothes he had worn during the voyage. With the seamen in so ugly a mood he felt safer in that rig, one in which he would escape notice. He passed the Old Dock, turned left into Paradise Street, came into Whitechapel and turned left again into Dale Street. There he began to ask questions of passers-by, his inquiries finally leading him to a house on the left which was clearly marked "Preston, Steere & Andros" and then, in smaller letters "Agents." It was the right place but the building seemed deserted, with boards nailed over the ground-floor windows. Richard went on down towards Castle Street and presently found a respectable looking citizen to whom he could turn for information. "Preston, Steere & Andros?" he repeated.

"There is only the one partner now, old Mr Andros, but he was one of those who proposed to lower the seamen's rate of pay. I believe he has fled, boarding his windows up before they could be broken. A timorous man, old Mr Andros—he must be over eighty now—I heard tell that he was gone—he and his son, both—but whether to Warrington or Chester I couldn't say. A tight-fisted man, by repute, but I never did business with him myself."

Richard thanked this informant and walked on towards the Exchange, feeling now thoroughly downcast. He was alone and friendless in a strange town, a boy who had seldom been out of Guernsey, without employment or lodging and with only a few shillings in his purse. He asked several other strangers if they knew where old Mr Andros had gone but he soon came to suspect that his great-uncle was in a relatively small way of business, not very generally known or liked. It was also obvious that the

Liverpool merchants had other things to think about. Near the Exchange they were standing about in groups, talking quietly and exchanging anxious looks. If there were no immediate signs of disorder it was clear that further trouble was expected. From talk he overheard he concluded that all other ships in the port had been unrigged by the seamen and prevented from sailing. There was also some mention of enlisting and arming special constables, any reference to this plan being cut short when he was seen to be listening. He ran off in some confusion and made his way back to the *Charlotte*—all the home he had, his last tenuous link with Guernsey.

That evening he had a further talk with Mr Crosbie, who gave him leave to sleep on board the brig for another two nights, after which she was going into dry dock.

"I don't like the look of things, son," said Mr Crosbie. "I think the merchants will have to give in over the seamen's pay. After all a bargain is a bargain. But they'll try to get their own back by putting the ringleaders in prison. Then there'll be real trouble and you had best keep out of it."

"I heard something ashore about the arming of special constables."

"I heard that story too and it sounds all too likely. Once the firing starts we don't know how it will end. The one thing certain is that Liverpool is full of firearms, powder and shot. They export arms from here, brought by canal from Birmingham, much of the poorer stuff being for the slave trade. If firing begins this town is going to suffer."

All was quiet next day and it was said that the dispute was over. That evening, however, a crowd of sailors gathered outside the Exchange. Told to disperse, they refused and were fired on by the special constables. Richard heard the firing from a distance but kept clear of the town centre. He made further inquiries that day and eventually managed to track down Mr Gosfield, the clerk who had retired at the beginning of the month after working with Mr Andros for a quarter of a century. He lived in Bath Street, not far from the fort, a widower with a taste for gardening. He doubted very much whether Mr Andros would appoint another clerk, even supposing that he could be found and even assuming that commerce in Liverpool were to revive.

"What about young Mr Andros?"

"He'll sell that business as soon as his father retires. He married a wife with money—one of the Blundell family. Now you must look at my hollyhocks . . . Did you ever see the likes? I don't even water them . . ."

Round Water Street and St Nicholas Church there were signs of anxious activity among the merchants and shopkeepers, with windows being boarded up and doors barricaded. Richard came back to the brig that evening, his last, and wondered where he was to sleep the following night. He had little money left and nowhere to go, his only consolation being that the weather was warm. He took note of the stables near the Salthouse Dock and went out of his way to make friends with a stable boy called Pete. After helping Pete feed the horses, he promised to help again next day. By then, he hoped, there might be a chance to sleep in the hay-loft and find an odd corner for his bundle of clothes. Pete was not a very responsive character but he yielded in the end to a bribe of twopence. By the following day, 30 August, Richard had his corner of the hay-loft but realised that his tenancy was insecure. There were stable men to whom Pete was ancillary and a foreman above them again. With the port closed down these were not much in evidence but a resumption of work on the quayside would bring them back in force.

While Richard helped with the buckets and hay he was aware of noises from the town, trampling and smashing and at one moment the sound of cheering. Seamen were breaking into the premises of Mr Parr, the gunsmith. By midday many of the rioters were armed with muskets and a body of them could be seen coming down to the quayside. Richard and Pete watched this movement, unable to guess its 12-pounders from the *Derby,* which was in the Old Dock, and may have intended to land some more. It was not, however, as easy a task as all that, the gun barrels being slung from the main yard-arm and the gun-trucks manhandled over an improvised gangway. By now the seamen had convinced themselves that they were soldiers, some having assumed rank as captain or colonel and one, indeed, as general. The more drunken of them were holding an unsteady sort of parade with much saluting and shouting of orders. Once they had the two cannon reassembled there was nothing to prevent their pushing them into battle. But a vague idea of doing things in military style led them to conclude that their cannon should be horse-drawn and that they needed two cartloads of ammunition. A party of rioters headed, therefore, towards the stables from which Pete and Richard were watching the riot. These men were mostly sober but had only a vague idea of stable practice. Brushing Pete aside, who screamed his protests, they tried to harness the eight horses they had decided to take. A confused scene followed, with much cursing and neighing, the sailors increasingly frustrated and the horses at once annoyed and alarmed. Backed into a corner with Pete and armed with a pitchfork, Richard heard snatches of dialogue—"Dammit, Joe, I can't rig this jib-sheet!"—"It's upside down, mate, but what do I do with this down-haul?"—"Put that away, you fool—a cart-horse doesn't need a saddle."—"Hell—this blasted horse trod on me foot!"—"Lucky we aren't in the cavalry."—"Well, here's one horse under a jury rig, all knotted and spliced. What next, sergeant?" Nearest Richard was a large grey horse which five seamen were trying to harness. One of them dropped a strap on the ground and bent over to pick it up. Seizing his opportunity the grey bit him in the buttocks, bringing the operation to a standstill. The wounded man limped away amidst laughter but the others stood back from the horse and scratched their heads. One of them, turning round, saw Richard and had an inspiration. "Come here, boy!" he shouted. "*You* rig this beast or I'll cut your liver out!" All eight horses were then harnessed by Pete, with Richard's help, and led out to where the cannon stood on the quayside. The carts were then pushed out and loaded and the cannon hitched to each cart-tail. The rioters' battery was ready to go into action.

Richard now thought that his part in the campaign was over, and Pete's only wish was to tell the foreman what had happened, but neither was to escape so easily. They were told to stay with the horses. As the "sergeant" said, "We must have someone who can tell the bow from the stern." The result was that the boys were made to take their place in the column of march, committed to a wild operation which could lead, as likely as not, to the gallows. Somewhere ahead in the column Richard could glimpse a flag and from the same direction came the beat of a drum. The word to march was passed down the ranks and the advance began, with Richard's gun leading. The distance to be covered was small, being little more than half the length of Castle Street. At that point the head of the army came under fire from the Exchange, the special constables shooting from the windows. The advance halted and the word came back to bring up the artillery. There was wild and ineffective musketry practice on

either side but the cannon were brought forward, Richard finding himself under fire for the first time. "Wheel to starboard!"
he yelled, pulling the horses' heads round.

"What, running away?" shouted a bystander, but Richard persisted.

"Come *on!*" he cried and swung the cart round. This brought
the cannon into position with its muzzle towards the Exchange,
its cart in rear and the horses behind that again. The sailors
cheered, cast off the lashing and loaded the gun. To their left the
other gun was dragged into line with more difficulty, neither Pete
nor anyone else realising that a 180-degree turn was needed to
bring the gun into action. Then there was a hitch. There was no
lighted match, no means of firing the cannon. Richard looked
wildly round and saw that smoke was coming from a chimney
on his right. "In there!" he shouted and a group of sailors charged
Mr Warren's front door and broke into his parlour. A minute
later one of them came out with a live coal carried in the tongs.
"Stand back!" thundered the self-appointed gunner. "I'm going
to take aim!" He fussed over this for a minute while the man
with the coal blew on it. There were a number of potential loot-
ers sheltering in doorways and one of them called out in derision,
"Aim at the Goose!" He pointed to the heraldic cormorant carved
on the pediment of the Exchange. Why the gunner should have
heeded this advice must remain a mystery but he did so, telling
his mates to elevate. They knocked out the quoin and stood
back. "Fire!" shouted the gunner and the live coal was applied
to the touch-hole. There was a noise like the crack of doom, followed at once by the crash of broken glass.

Where that first shot went was anyone's guess, but the effect
of the blast was dramatic. In the confined space of that narrow
street the shock was enough to destroy every window in sight

and quite a few in the streets adjacent. The nearer front doors were blown in, the shutters unhinged, the roof slates loosened and some chimney-pots brought down. This surprising result was enough in itself to explain the eighteenth-century reluctance to use cannon in street-fighting. Even the rioters were a little surprised to see the results of that first cannon shot. The second followed, from the other gun, but the shock had negligible effect on buildings already windowless. As for the musketry, it caused relatively few casualties on either side. The rioters were unskilled, excited and under no sort of discipline. Their opponents were little better—clerks and labourers hired at ten shillings a day. When the rioters gave up their original plan of attack, they left the Exchange bullet-scarred but impregnable, and turned instead to the easier and more satisfying task of sacking the houses of their particular enemies—Mr Thomas Ratcliffe, Mr William James and Mr John Simmons. As they dispersed to do this, the crowd in Castle Street thinned out considerably and the firing died away. Richard asked the remaining sailors to help him lead the horses back to their stables. They agreed to do this, leaving the cannon deserted on the stricken field, and the withdrawal began. Turning to the right beside the Old Dock, however, Richard walked into a group of special constables who must have come round by the Goree Causeway. Pete made his escape, running round the head of the Dock into Hanover Street, but Richard's struggles were in vain. He was held fast by two armed men and led with other prisoners towards Liverpool Tower, the old gaol on the riverside. He argued as he went:

"I'm not one of the rioters," Richard protested, "I was just saving the horses!"

"Tell that to the court, my lad."

"But I'm a stranger here, just landed from Guernsey. I'm not even a sailor."

"Then why are you dressed like one?"

"That's no crime. I'm *not* a rioter!"

At this point there was an interruption, a bystander calling out: "Pay no need to that blarney! He was the boy who helped turn the cannon. I saw him! Yes, and he told the gunner where to find a match."

Richard's protests died away as he realised that what this witness said was very nearly the truth. He knew at the same instant that fifty other people might have seen him beside that cannon. He must have been mad! But what possessed him to help the rioters? He had no sympathy for their stupidities, he hated the sight of wanton destruction and yet, somehow, he had wanted to see that gun properly handled. He had given no thought to the question of where the shot would go, perhaps causing injury or death. He had at that moment discovered something new about himself; that he hated to see incompetence. If there was a gun to be fired—even by an enemy—he would still rather it were done properly. It was a moment of self-revelation, so interesting that he said not a word more until the gaol was reached. The outer door opened, he was led along a corridor, then to the left. A cell door was unlocked and he and two other men were thrust into a poorly-lit cell with some straw on the stone flags and a wooden bucket as its only article of furniture. The door slammed and the retreating footsteps were soon inaudible. His first great adventure in the world at large, his first visit to this great seaport, had ended with him in prison, not only charged or about to be charged with riotous behaviour but knowing with certainty that the charges could be proved. He was guilty and he knew it. It only remained for him to hear the sentence.

Of the other two prisoners who shared the cell, one was evidently drunk. After being sick on the floor, missing the bucket, he fell asleep on the straw. The other seaman was a morose fellow called Will with a grudge against society. Richard asked him timidly what sentence they might expect.

"Sentence, mate! What would *you* do to men who had frightened the life out of you, brought your business to a halt, made you all look foolish, and drove you into granting what they asked at first? What would *you* do? Let them off? No, mate, you'd rig the noose at the yard-arm. And that, youngster, is what will be happening tomorrow."

"What, to be hanged just for—for—what we d-did?"

"And why not, boy? When did sailors ever get justice, let alone mercy? I tell you, these merchants are scared and some of us will have to pay for it."

"But there were hundreds in the riot—thousands, maybe— they couldn't hang us all, could they?"

"They haven't *caught* them all. Most will escape all right but you and I didn't. We are laid by the heels. You and I, that other fellow and a few more. We are the unlucky ones and that's for sure. Say your prayers, boy, while you can."

As evening came and the daylight faded a turnkey opened the door and pushed in three slices of bread and three mugs of water. He vanished again without saying a word but Richard could hear the other doors being opened and shut. Then the noise died away and he ate his bread and tasted the water. He lay down on the straw and tried to sleep but it was hours, seemingly, before sleep would come. After that he had nightmares, seeing himself already in the dock but unable to say a word in his own defence. He had the answer—more than that, he had an alibi—but the words would not come. "So," said the judge, "you have nothing to say?" He was dumb and could only watch in horror while the judge put on his black cap. . . . He woke with a scream and was cursed by the morose man for waking him. He then slept some more and it was daylight. There was breakfast of bread and water and the long morning passed. At midday each prisoner had a plateful of some unmentionable and coldish stew. Then it was evening again but with the fading light came noises which heralded more company on the way. Doors opened and slammed, the sound coming nearer until their own door was opened in its turn. Another man was thrust into their cell, the door shut and other doors opened and closed in the distance, the sound dying away until all was silent.

The newcomer, called Tom, was younger than Richard's other two companions and much more talkative. "The fun's all over now," he moaned. "D'you know what? They brought in a whole regiment of dragoons—Lord Pembroke's dragoons from Manchester. We had to run and we had to hide, some in attics and some in cellars. It weren't no good, though, for people who saw us told the troopers. 'This way, sergeant,' they said, 'and down them stairs.' We hadn't a chance, I tell you, and few there were what even made a fight of it."

"Where did *you* hide?" asked Richard.

"Me? I hid in a cellar under some tarpaulin big as a hatch cover. That'll do the trick, I said to myself, for nobody had seen me. A trooper looked in, too, and told the officers there was no one there. 'You haven't looked,' said the ensign and he stuck his sword through the tarpaulin, missing me by about a foot. I didn't wait for him to do it again but called out 'I'm here, you lubber, and keep that tooth-pick away from me.' They had me then, and I was a prisoner. So is every other seaman they clapped eyes on.

Those dragoons didn't miss much, I tell you, and here I am in the bilboes. It was fun while it lasted but the fun's over now."

"What do you think will happen to us?" asked Richard.

"Damned if I know. But I hear that press warrants have been issued and officers sent up from London. We may be given the choice between the navy and Lancaster Gaol."

"And I'd choose the gaol," said Will. "I have had both and the navy's the worse. Reefing the topsails in a freezing gale! Racing down the shrouds with a dozen at the gangway for the last man down! There's no fun here but at least the gaol won't sink."

"There's the grog, though," argued Tom. "And in wartime there's the chance of prize-money. I knew a man who made six guineas once out of a French prize that didn't even fire more than a broadside. His cruise ashore was something to talk about!"

"The New England men won't be worth catching," replied the morose Will. "They sail like greased lightning and fight like fury and are worthless at the end of it."

The third man, who had been sick, contributed nothing to this conversation or any other. He belched once or twice but that was all. As for Richard, he shuddered at the thought of being in gaol for any length of time. As against that, he had to recognise that the risk of the gaol capsizing was comparatively remote. Which would he choose if offered the choice? Then he reflected that the decision, most probably, would not be his. Thinking thus, Richard slept once more for a while, only to be woken as the door of the cell was unlocked again. The turnkey had a lantern by the light of which he could see that another prisoner was being thrust in, a smallish man with long hair and a long-tailed coat, no seaman and no very convincing rioter. Richard had only a glimpse of the man before the door slammed, leaving him again in darkness.

Chapter 2

SCENE ON MERSEYSIDE

"WAKE UP!" The words came in a strangled scream. "WAKE UP!" It was still pitch dark and Richard was being shaken by a fellow prisoner, evidently the last arrival. "Wake up for pete's sake!" After a pause came the explanation: "I daren't go to sleep in case I dream again."

"You had a nightmare, sir?" asked Richard sleepily and without much real interest.

"It was terrible, terrible! I was about to be thrown into a pond teeming with crocodiles, their scales shining, their jaws open, their teeth . . . King George had ordered it and was there to see it done."

"So you wake, sir, to something a little better."

"But quite horrible enough."

"You were arrested as a rioter?"

"Yes, but I played no part in the riot. I did not cause it, I'll swear. I did nothing to encourage it. I had no part in it, none. I was there merely to report what took place."

"You were there, you mean, on behalf of the press?"

"I am assistant editor of the *Clarion Call*."

This statement was made impressively but Richard, who had never heard of that periodical—or any other published outside Guernsey—pursued a policy of caution.

"Then you will be released, sir, no doubt, when it is known who you are?"

"Don't you believe it, boy. The *Clarion Call* is a radical weekly, its editorials hostile to the government, its mere existence deplored by all in authority. Paid witnesses will appear against me, no doubt of it. I shall be charged with treason. I may be sent to Botany Bay. I may have, for that matter, but a few short days to live."

"But you won't be thrown to the crocodiles."

"The more's the pity, as some folk would say. Hanging, they would agree, is too good for me. The truth is, young man, that I have been a thorn in their side for years."

"Perhaps you might try to give less offence?"

"And betray the cause of the common people? Never while I live! But I suffer for the people's sake, for I dare not sleep. I dare not face the crocodile's teeth. So please be so good as to keep me awake. Talk to me about anything that comes into your head. Tell me what you think of Liverpool. Better still, tell me the story of your life. You are honest, young man, I feel sure of that. No government spy, you are loyal to the working folk among whom you live. You are no friend, surely, to the tyrants who rule this land? Tell me, first, where you were born and when. Tell me, finally, how you came to be in this prison."

"Very well, sir. Mine is too dull a story, however, to keep you awake for long. It begins in October 1760, a few days after the late king died, when I was born in St Peter Port, Guernsey. I was christened Richard Andros and my surname is Delancey."

"A French name?"

"French Huguenot, sir. I am the descendant of a noble family. Andros is my mother's name, well known in Guernsey. My father is a corn chandler but in only a small way of business."

"Brought up in poverty, you should be on my side against the government."

"No, sir. I am a gentleman."

"The son of a small tradesman?"

"My father is a gentleman by birth, learning some Latin and well able to keep accounts. He married into a family of great former wealth. Amias Andros was bailiff of Guernsey under Charles II, and his son, Sir Edmund, was governor of New York and Virginia. James Andros was colonel in the Militia and seigneur of Anneville. My mother's relatives did not approve of my mother's marriage and will scarcely speak to my father, not even when they buy their oats and hay from him. Sir Edmund was once major in Prince Rupert's Dragoons and my mother wished to name me Rupert. My father would not have that and I was called after my mother's uncle, Richard Andros, a shipowner here in Liverpool and the only one of her relatives to take notice of her. He is my godfather and I came here to see him. I had two elder brothers, Mathew and Michael, and have an elder sister called Rachel. We were brought up in an old house overlooking the harbour, and spent our time fishing and sailing, in the end, an old and crazy boat which Mathew had somehow come to own. We all learnt to read and write and father taught us arithmetic, geometry and book-keeping. Both my brothers went to sea, Mathew ending as third mate in a collier out of Sunderland. He was drowned when she went ashore off Yarmouth in a fog. Michael went to the East Indies and we have never heard of him since. I also meant to be a seaman and have learnt something of navigation from an old merchant skipper, but my mother, after Michael's being seemingly lost, would have none of it. She wants me to find work in a shipowner's counting-house and wrote about this to my great-uncle in Liverpool."

"Did he promise you a place?"

"He did indeed and I have his letter in my pocket."

"Will you be glad to work in your great-uncle's office?"

"I don't think so but there is reason, I suppose, in keeping a third son ashore after two others have been lost at sea. Had I the chance, I should go to sea. I had never thought of any other calling."

"And is your uncle ready to employ you?"

"He has left town, sir, and his business seems to be at a stand-still. So it may happen that I must go to sea after all. What else is there to do?"

"But it will not be easy to find a berth."

"I know that, sir."

"What brought you here, then?"

Richard explained the circumstances that had led to his arrest, adding the almost tearful conclusion that he meant no harm:

"But I'm guilty, sir," he concluded, "of taking part in the riot. I was there and people saw me."

"You should be proud of what you did and now, after being thrown into prison, you should be on the side of the people. You should be against the government. As a Guernseyman, you speak French?"

"Why, yes, sir."

"So you and your neighbours should sympathise with the Frenchmen who brought about their monarchy's downfall!"

"Folk in Guernsey have no liking, sir, for French atheists. Many Guernseymen are followers, you see, of Mr John Wesley."

"Are you a Wesleyan, then?"

"Not me, sir, I'm a gentleman."

"Even in prison?"

"I'm still a Delancey and still an Andros on my mother's side."

A quiet and desultory conversation continued for another hour or so without disturbing the other prisoners. Richard spoke

at length about his family and friends, about the likelihood of
his sister marrying John Sedley, a coming man in Bristol, about
his father's recent illness and consistent lack of success in business and about his mother's determination that one at least of
her children should regain the position in society to which his
gentle birth entitled him. Then he spoke of his own prospects.
He was not a real seaman as yet, as he freely admitted, not being
used to working aloft. He could hand, reef and steer, though,
and even take an altitude. Surely there would be a berth for him
and perhaps a career? There was no reply and Richard realised
that his radical friend had fallen asleep, having long since lost
interest in what Richard was saying. This was hardly surprising,
as Richard told himself, in that his life story was so far of no
real interest to anyone. But the dull narrative had served one
purpose at least, for the radical scribbler had seemingly dreamt
no more about crocodiles. When first light penetrated the barred
windows the journalist was revealed as a poor misshapen crea-
ture, almost a hunchback, shabbily dressed and with ink-stained
shirtsleeves. While he and the others slept Richard thought
deeply about his future, assuming hopefully that he would escape
the gallows. Should he try again to find his great-uncle? Should
he ask his great-uncle's help in seeking employment with another
shipowner? In trying to decide upon a plan, he pulled out his
great-uncle's letter and read it under the window. It was dated
from Dale Street on 11 October 1774, and the most significant
passage read: "It so befalls that the worthy Mr Gosfield, my oldest clerk, plans his retirement for the First of August next
year, twenty-five years to the day since he first entered my
employ. He will be succeeded by Mr Lock, whose place in turn
will be filled by Mr Henderson. That last promotion will leave
the junior position vacant and I shall be pleased to offer that to

my great-nephew, not as a permanency nor with anything more than a modest remuneration but in the expectation that he will soon prove his worth and justify your hopes in him. You must suppose that I am myself these days a somewhat passive partner in the firm but my son, Edmund, is fully apprized of the arrangement I propose and will be kindly disposed towards his cousin."

Richard could remember the conversation which followed the reading of this letter at table. His mother commented at once on her uncle's benevolence:

"You see, Mr Delancey, that we are not wholly forgot by all our relatives. This is a kind response to my letter."

His father, less impressed, asked how long it was since great-uncle Richard last wrote? It then appeared that his last letter was the one in which he agreed to stand godfather to his great-nephew, a letter written some fourteen years before. His mother pointed out that her uncle had been a very busy man, employing as many as three clerks and managing three or four vessels at the least. When consulted, young Richard himself expressed a preference for the sea but against this his mother was adamant, urging every reason but the real one. She pleaded that a clerkship in a shipowner's counting-house must be thought a very eligible place. Nor need Richard think himself a landsman for he might have much occasion to be aboard ship and could even some day become agent in a foreign port. Talking with Rachel afterwards, Richard had said of his great-uncle that the old skinflint had ignored his poor relatives for fourteen years and that now, when business was slack, he saw the chance to replace his junior clerk by an almost unpaid office boy. But the whole situation had changed since the letter was written. No agreement had been reached with the American colonies and England was evidently on the brink of war. He had done his best to see his godfather and had satisfied himself that a clerkship in some other shipping office would be difficult or impossible to obtain. Now he had the chance to go against his parents' wishes without actually disobeying them. Try as he might, he could not do what he had been told to do.

When his journalist friend, whose name turned out to be Elisha Crabtree, woke up, Richard told him that he had more or less decided against an office career. It soon appeared that Mr Crabtree remembered not a word of all that Richard had told him. To him Richard was no more than the voice which kept him awake but which had finally lulled him to sleep. He showed his gratitude only in a final effort to make Richard a radical. A slightly acrimonious argument followed in which the grown man had no difficulty in besting a mere boy. He made no convert, however, and ended on an unfriendly note.

"I'll tell you what it is, my young friend. You are penniless and in gaol, without a trade and without any prospects. Somehow, for all that, you have come to believe that you are a gentleman, that you deserve to have a fortune, a manor house, a carriage and servants. You have no thought for others who are as penniless as you are, as friendless and as unskilled. You have no sympathy for the common people, oppressed as we all are by the tyrants who rule this unhappy land. You are, I fear, of a breed not unknown among us, the men who feel cheated of some imagined fortune to which they were never entitled, the men with pretensions and little else. These are ruthless, dangerous men, ready for treason, stratagems and spoils—treason against the working multitude, I mean—men who live and may die by the sword."

"Men like Francis Drake?" Richard suggested hopefully but

the other prisoners, led by Tom, had come to the end of their patience. "Pipe down, you two!" they shouted. "Stop chattering and let us have some peace and quiet!" Quiet lasted until the midday meal arrived.

Later that day the cell door was thrown open and a grey-haired naval lieutenant walked in, accompanied by a turnkey. He looked without enthusiasm at the unshaven and dirty occupants of the cell. Then he pointed at Tom and said, "That one." He hesitated for a moment and added, pointing at Richard, "Yes, the boy as well." He walked out again and the turnkey said roughly, "Come on, you two. Rise and shine!" They obeyed, Tom with some reluctance, and found themselves in the custody of some armed seamen collected in the corridor. They were marched from cell to cell while the lieutenant chose a few more men, about ten in all. These were then collected in a courtyard where the lieutenant made a short speech to them, terse and very much to the point:

"Listen, men, you have been taken up as rioters and will presently be charged with that offence before the mayor and aldermen. All they can do is to commit you for trial at the next Assizes. While awaiting that trial you may be pressed into the navy, which may save you from hanging—which, by the way, is what you deserve. It is nothing to me whether you hang or not but it so happens that the cutter *Seaflower* is here in the river and can accept a few volunteers on passage to London. His Majesty has not yet put the navy on a war footing but we are having trouble, as you know, with some misguided folk in America. Some good seamen are wanted, but as *volunteers,* I repeat. This is a service to which any man must be proud to belong. Mr Huggins!" The lieutenant lost all interest in the proceedings at this moment and walked away, his place being taken by a burly petty officer, who proceeded to make what was evidently a set speech.

"Now's your chance, men, to volunteer for the king's service where merit is always rewarded and where the active get promotion. Do well and you may be an officer in a year or two, maybe with a handle to your name. Don't skulk ashore, men, or work in a collier, doing nothing for yourself and being kicked around by others. Go on board a man-of-war and become a proper seaman, make prize-money, sing and dance, drink grog and have all the girls in love with you. This is your chance and there mayn't be another. Who'll volunteer? Don't all speak at once but let's see who'll be first."

Driven by an impulse he could not explain and for which he was soon to curse himself, Richard stepped forward and spoke like a man:

"I'll join."

Chapter 3

CAPTAIN'S CLERK

THE RECEIVING SHIP *Rainbow*, built as long ago as 1747, was moored off Woolwich, not far from where she had originally been built. As the men came through her main entry they were first examined by the surgeon, who rejected the lame, the halt and the blind. Those found acceptable were then confronted by the master-at-arms who asked each in turn his name, his age and his trade. Seated at a table behind him, Mr Farley, the purser's clerk, entered these bare facts in a ledger. Some of the names given were probably assumed but nobody cared about that. The name entered, whether true or false, would be the man's name until he might be discharged. The ages given were also approximate and seldom provoked any discussion unless patently false. Most of the men being entered at this stage of the war were seamen but many tried to qualify their entry under this heading, giving a description of the work they had previously done. One had been in the sailmaker's crew, another had been coxswain, a third claimed—amidst some laughter—to have been captain of the head. A lieutenant standing in the background made a swift decision in each doubtful case and the volunteers were mostly entered as able or ordinary seamen or, in one instance, as volunteer second class. When Richard's turn came he described himself as "clerk" aged seventeen and was entered as a landsman.

"Do you want any help?" he asked Mr Farley, who looked surprised. "I'll let you know if I do," he replied shortly, looking up from his book and then turning to make the next entry: Tom Yates, recent inmate of Liverpool town gaol, who ranked as able seaman.

Later that evening Farley sent for Richard and told him that he would be given a chance to demonstrate his usefulness. There was a great deal of work to do, entering, paying and kitting out the men as they entered and Richard found himself writing and copying for dear life. He thought at first that he had been a fool to join the navy at all. He wondered, at the same time, whether he had not made a false move in offering to help with the paper-work. He had wanted originally to go to sea and here he was turning aside from the line of duty which would have made him a seaman. He knew well enough why he had done it. Will, his dour cell mate, had talked of a captain who would flog the last man down from the rigging. If that were he his only plan, he had decided, would be to throw himself overboard. But he might be picked up, even then. . . . No, a clerk's position would save him from the worst and he could change later, perhaps, to a more active role. Whether he could be shipped as clerk was another matter, depending upon Mr Farley. Aiming to please that immediate superior, he came near to making himself indispens-able, which would have kept him in the *Rainbow* for ever. He was lucky in one respect, however, that he had been able to recover his bundle from the Salthouse Dock stables, where the taciturn Pete had actually looked after it. He was thus enabled to look the part, having still a spare suit which he could offer to Farley as a gift. He did this only after he had found a suc-cessor, a worthy clerk from Aberdeen who was avoiding the possible consequences of bigamy. The result was, eventually, a recommendation to the purser of the *Romney* of 50 guns, a fourth-rate ship built in 1762; an old example of what was becoming an obsolete class. She was being fitted for sea but was not yet in commission, the work on board being divided between the purser, the gunner, the boatswain and the carpenter. Although still entered as "landsman" Richard was, in fact, the purser's clerk, with plenty to do in correspondence and in the checking and listing of stores. The purser was a middle-aged man called Weaver whose home was in Woolwich and who was using every opportunity to improve and furnish it at the expense of the Navy Board. Men from the carpenter's crew were always being sent off on mysterious errands with boatloads of timber, cordage, and paint. Richard was necessarily privy to these transactions and was given small sums to ensure his silence. During the course of that winter he accumulated quite a useful sum of money and came to the conclusion that everyone on board had been doing much the same. He finally provided himself with clothes modelled on those worn by the purser: blue serge coat and hat of vaguely naval pattern with white breeches and waistcoat. He might not as yet be much of a man-of-war's man but a Woolwich tailor did something to make him at least look the part.

On a freezing day in February 1776 the *Romney* was commissioned by young Captain George Davenport, a cousin, it was said, of Lord Tiverton. Looking elegant but very cold, he read his commission to what ship's company there was and vanished again. His place was soon taken, however, by Lieutenant Garland. From the moment of his arrival as first lieutenant, discipline began to be enforced. With the appearance of Lieutenant Simon the effort began to collect a crew. There was no great shortage at this stage, only good men being accepted, and most of these came from the receiving ships. At Richard's instigation the purser asked the first lieutenant whether anyone had been chosen as captain's clerk. As none had been named, Richard was given the acting appointment—the purser being glad to lose someone who knew too much—and was well established when the captain finally took up his duties. There was a tense moment for Richard when the captain first examined him and inspected his handwriting. Apparently satisfied, the captain asked a final question which took Richard completely by surprise:

"Are you related to Oliver de Lancey of the 17th Dragoons?"

Richard knew of no relatives on his father's side but quickly took his chance.

"A distant cousin, sir."

His respectability thus established, Richard now became a member of the midshipmen's mess. He had come a long way since the time of his visit to Liverpool Gaol.

Members of the gunroom mess included master's mates, midshipmen, the surgeon's mate, the captain's clerk, and some boys, one or two of them vaguely classed as "captain's servant." Ages ranged from thirty down to about thirteen, a common characteristic most of these young men shared being an allowance from their fathers, without which they could not have paid their mess bills. A volunteer first class was thus regarded as a floating medium between something and nothing, paid about a farthing an hour, sleeping or waking. The captain's clerk, like the surgeon's mate, was rather more generously paid and could just manage, if careful, without help from home. He was fortunate in another way for he actually had a cabin in the steerage; not one of the best, to be sure, but better than a hammock in the cockpit. He was fortunate again in being one of the "idlers" who kept no watch. As against that, he had not the remotest chance of reaching the higher ranks of the service. He was inferior, in that respect, to the youngest boy in the gunroom mess.

Once the *Romney* was manned the previous confusion turned to apparent chaos, the decks being covered with spars, ropes, barrels, tar-buckets and paint-pots. Fitting out the ship for sea called for multifarious efforts and continual noise, hammering, banging, squeaking and shouting. Richard was lucky at least in two respects. In the first place he had been on board the ship long enough to have made himself familiar with it so that if not a real seaman he at least knew the ropes. In the second place he had work to do and was thus spared the novice's feeling of being useless and in the way. Captain Davenport's air of languid gentility was deceptive as Richard soon found, and concealed an impressive capacity for work. There was a daunting volume of correspondence with the Navy Board, with the dockyard, with the Ordnance Department, the Victualling Department, the receiving ships, the Admiralty and the flagship. Every letter of importance had to be sent in duplicate or triplicate, with copies for information and a final copy in a letter-book. Working quickly himself, he spared nobody else, afloat or ashore, and Richard least of all. As for the warrant officers, they were driven to despair by his passion for detail. Richard inevitably heard snatches of conversation not intended for his ears. "You are to remember, Mr Evans, that we may be in battle within three months from today. Our lives may depend upon what we do now." But what could the captain mean? We were at war after a fashion but the rebels had practically no men-of-war. What serious fighting could there be? He would have liked to discuss the question with his messmates but he knew that this was something he had to avoid. The more he knew the less he could talk.

While discreet in conversation, Richard felt able to express himself more freely in a letter to his parents. He told them that he was captain's clerk in the *Romney* and ranked almost as mid-shipman. Rumour had it that they were bound for America. All were in good heart but sorry to be fighting their kinsfolk rather than their natural enemies, the French and the Spanish.

Early in April the *Romney* sailed for Spithead where the fleet for America was collecting. When Captain Davenport ordered the anchor to be dropped the ships in sight seemed innumerable, most of them transports and some of them fitted for carrying horses. There were men-of-war in addition and it soon transpired that the *Eagle,* Captain Duncan, was to be the flagship and that Lord Howe was to be the admiral. All was activity as far as the eye could see, the sea alive with boats going back and forth and the sun gleaming on new paintwork and well-scrubbed decks. Richard was thrilled at the sight, which was new to him, and proud to think that he played some part in a great enterprise. He began again to regret his civilian role, to wish that he could some day wear a sword. But how could that be possible? The captain would expect some payment and he, as a volunteer, would need an allowance. There would be the problem of finding another captain's clerk, and there was none on board who could do the work. There was no money, anyway, and he must forget the possibility. His mind went back to it, nevertheless, and the more so in that his work had dwindled somewhat after the ship sailed.

He was on deck more now and could watch the midshipmen's antics in the rigging. As he did so one day he noticed that one boy called Jim Ridley seemed to have more energy than the rest, still eager to race when the others had tired of the game and gone below. Still flushed from playing follow-my-leader, Jim ran up to Richard crying "Race you to the main-topmasthead and down! Come on, inkstains. I'll give you to the maintop!"

"Done!" said Richard, rather to his own surprise and sprang to the weather rigging.

As he went up hand over hand he remembered that he must use the futtock shrouds, not the lubber's hole, and wondered whether he could make it. He had been aloft before but only in London River, not with the masts swaying dizzily like this. With an effort of will he reached the maintop and, glancing down, saw that Jim had started. He threw himself at the topmast shrouds and began to climb, feeling short of breath but keen at least to finish the race. Touching the topmasthead he began the scramble down, passing Jim who was gaining fast on the way up, reached the maintop again, tackled the futtocks (this time without noticing them) and finally made the deck with a few seconds to spare. Gasping, he met the eyes of the first lieutenant who had evidently watched the race from the quarterdeck.

"Well enough for an idler," he said, "but who will write the letters after you've broken your neck?" This could have been a reproof but Richard thought that the tone was friendly.

"Well done, Dick," said his opponent. "Next time, we'll start even!"

A few days later Richard received a letter dated 15 April 1776 from his mother and expressing the opinion that he would be better as midshipman while a long war offered chance of promotion. The letter ended with better news from home:

"You will be glad to know that your father's business is prospering better this year, he being appointed to supply forage to the enlarged garrison, the officers chargers and artillery and transport. He is often poorly these days but cheer'd to be out of debt and more in repute among the townsfolk. How content we should be to place our son on the quarterdeck if we knew how to bring it about. Rachel is not yet married but will be so in June or July, she sends her love so does your father who is too busy to write but wd much like to see you before you go overseas but we all see that there is little chance of it. May God bless your voyage and keep you from danger at sea and in battle.

With love from us all,
Mother

Postscript. I told Robert Le Huray once your schoolfellow that you were clerk in a man-of-war, he said to tell you that he wd like such a place if you shd heere of another, he being discontent with being clerk to Mr Falla."

Re-reading this, Richard realised that war would certainly bring business to a forage merchant—as, for example, to those doing business round Portsmouth who must be at their wits' end to supply the transports. His father's business had likewise improved, but a strengthening of the garrison in Guernsey would seem to suggest the likelihood of war with France (an idea that was new to him). Knowing that the purser had been over to visit several of the nearer transports, Richard asked him how they did for forage.

"Well, young man, you can see what their difficulty is. It takes weeks to assemble a convoy like this, 44 transports when all are present, and those here first will have used up much of their supplies while still at anchor. When the admiral makes the signal to weigh anchor, these will signal that they are short of provisions and forage."

Richard could see no end to this process but Lord Howe was an old hand, knowing the answer to this and every other problem. When he made the signal on 12 May there were protesting flags hoisted all round. He ignored them all and fired another gun, resolved to use a fair wind while it lasted. Showing obvious reluctance the convoy sailed, with men-of-war like sheepdogs, their guns barking at the stragglers. The voyage down Channel began and it brought with it, for Richard, the surprise of his life. At dinner on the 13th one of the master's mates, an "oldster" called Culling, remarked casually that the convoy was to anchor next day off St Peter Port. He had been told by the officer of the watch.

"Whatever for?" asked Tomlinson, the senior midshipman.

"It seems that the horse transports are short of forage."

"There might be a better reason," said Jim.

"Such as what?" inquired Culling.

"Dick lives there!" Jim revealed.

"What an odd place to live . . ." drawled midshipman Harcourt.

"It was a Guernseyman," said Richard, "who devised the uniform you hope to wear when you are commissioned."

"Oh rubbish. Guernseymen all wear that blue knitted garment which looks like a jersey but isn't."

"I wonder," said Richard, "whether the first lieutenant will let me go ashore?"

"But of course," replied Harcourt. "It's lucky that he has nothing else to think about."

The squadron and convoy dropped anchor off St Peter Port on 14 May and Dick was among those allowed on shore. He fairly ran to the Pollet but found several others ahead of him. The demand was for forage and Mr Delancey had barely time to greet his son before plunging into what seemed the trading boom of a lifetime.

"One at a time, please, gentlemen," he cried and was soon lost in quantities and sums.

Richard ran upstairs to see his mother and sister and was soon exchanging news and congratulations.

"I've been thinking, Richard," said his mother, "about your career in the navy. I don't want to see you a purser. I want you to be an officer like so many of your relatives. You might end as a captain—maybe as an admiral. We'll hope for peace, of course, but these misguided rebels are so ungrateful and stupid that a long war may be the result with opportunities for prize-money and promotion. When we heard that your ship was here we knew that it was by the disposition of providence. Your father will see Captain Davenport tomorrow."

Short as his absence had been, everyone was convinced that Richard had grown several inches and looked like the hero he was surely destined to be. When all had been said, Richard hurried back to the *Romney's* boat. He was not allowed to go ashore again.

Next day there was a final and frenzied scene with boats being laden with vegetables and flour bags, bales of hay and bundles of straw. Cows bellowed piteously as they were slung aboard transports, pigs squealed to heaven as they were pushed over the quay, to be followed into the boat by sacks of potatoes and barrels of wine. Amidst all this tumult a jollyboat came alongside the *Romney* with Mr Delancey in his best suit and cloak. Warned in advance, the officer of the watch welcomed him aboard and told Richard to show his father to the captain's cabin. Critical as he had to feel, Richard admitted to himself that Mr Delancey was at least looking the part, being better dressed than Richard had ever seen him. He knocked at the door, announced his father's arrival and promptly withdrew, keeping within earshot in case he should be wanted. The summons eventually came and he reported smartly, finding his father alone with the captain.

"Well, young man, you will be glad to hear that your transfer from the civilian to the military branch of the service has been agreed but on condition that I am supplied with another clerk. Your father foresaw this condition—with remarkable insight, sir, if I may say so—and has another youngster ready to come on board. Provided he is acceptable I am prepared to give you a new rating of captain's servant. You will have to learn another trade but the first lieutenant tells me that you are not without promise and that he has seen you aloft. Are you willing to be re-rated and at a lower rate of pay?"

"Aye, aye, sir—and thank you, sir."

"Then fetch this other youngster, Mr Delancey, and we'll have his dunnage aboard. We are to sail in two hours time and he with us unless he prove to be illiterate." Robert Le Huray passed the test, however, and Richard finally said goodbye to his father at the entry port.

"Many thanks, sir, I'll try to justify your faith in me. My hope is that you are not ruined in the meanwhile."

"Provided the war goes on, Richard, your allowance will be paid. If today's business were the average I could keep you in the Foot Guards! But we'd best aim lower and hope to see you a lieutenant, as befits a descendant of the Andros family."

"Or a de Lancey, sir. I told you of what Captain Davenport said."

"So you did, Richard, but I never heard of any such relative and won't dare claim your cavalryman as a cousin. But I see the whole of America as an Andros estate, waiting for you to take possession of it as rightful owner. There is a parcel for you in the boat alongside. When you have it, I must say goodbye and go ashore."

After waving as long as the boat was in sight, Richard hurried below and unpacked the parcel. It contained a length of blue cloth, some shirts and stockings, a sextant, Norie's *Seamanship* and a midshipman's dirk. He was still inspecting these when there was a knock on the door. "I'm sorry, Richard," said Robert Le Huray, "but I'm told that this is my cabin . . ." Richard said—untruthfully—that he didn't mind at all.

Richard began with a practical knowledge of boat-handling and some theoretical knowledge of navigation. To this he had added a knowledge of the ropes and of routine in a man-of-war. As from that point, his progress was slow. For one thing, he had begun too late, at sixteen instead of thirteen, and with no useful education to make up for the lost time. For another, he was less handy aloft than other boys of his age and had a tendency to feel sick and giddy. He was doggedly persevering in nautical astronomy but below average in his knots and splices. His best subject was gunnery but the *Romney* was a ship in which seamanship was regarded as more important—as indeed the most important thing in life. In the continual contest between the watches, evolutions timed by the stop-watch, he could only just hold his own. During the crossing of the Atlantic he daily regretted his change of status and loss of privacy but knew at the same time that he had burnt his boats. He must become a seaman or perish in the attempt. Aware of his limitations, his messmates were tolerant and often helpful. The junior lieutenants were more apt to single him out for ridicule and rebuke. So far as he was concerned, this was not, on the whole, a happy voyage.

Chapter 4

WARTIME NEW YORK

RICHARD had boldly claimed cousinship with the New York family of his name but his connection with them was difficult, in fact, to establish. The history of the American de Lanceys was easy to trace, on the other hand, for they were all descended from Etienne or Stephen de Lancey, a Huguenot gentleman of Caen in Normandy, who had migrated to England in 1686, went on to New York, married Anne Van Cortlandt and died in 1741, being buried in Trinity Church. Stephen had ten children in all, it seemed, three of them making a name for themselves. James was chief justice and at one time lieutenant-governor of New York. Peter, the squire of Westchester, married Elizabeth, daughter of Governor Cadwallader Colden, and came to own the Bowery Estate which he left to his eldest son, James. Oliver married Susannah, daughter of General Sir William Draper, and had several children including Stephen, a lawyer who married Cornelia, daughter of the Rev. H. Barclay of Trinity Church; Oliver, the cavalryman of whose existence Richard had been told; and Charlotte his younger sister. The wealth of the family was shared between the two cousins, James and Oliver. James's property in New York stretched for over a mile of waterfront on the East River, extending inland to Bowery Lane and centred upon De Lancey Square, next to Mr Rutger's property. Oliver was perhaps the richer of the two with a country house at Bloomingdale and important interests in New Jersey. The court or loyal or Church of England party in New York had been headed by the de Lanceys since the middle of the century, their family connections extending to the Drapers, Ludlows and Coldens, to Sir William Johnson, William Walton and John Watts. After the fall of New York theirs was, naturally, the party in power.

But where did Richard fit into this genealogy? He finally discovered that Etienne de Lancey of Caen had fathered a child in England before he sailed for America. This was John de Lancey, born 1689, whose son was Michael, a tradesman of Norwich and Richard's grandfather. It can be assumed that Michael's son, Mathew, fled to Guernsey as the result of some misconduct or scandal in early life. Richard learnt nothing about that. What he did discover was that Michael had died in 1737 when Mathew was aged two. That explained the broken tradition, but for which Richard would have known about his American relatives. On the face of it, Richard represented the elder branch of the family. As against that, it was a question whether John had been legitimate. Etienne could have married in about 1686–8, his wife dying before he left for America. It was also possible that he married only the once, John being the result of a more casual affair in London. Richard stood firmly by the theory of Etienne's first marriage and claimed cousinship with James, Oliver and the rest. From being a nobody of obscure origin on his father's side Richard could now regard himself as a fringe member of a very powerful clan. There was no question of his being adopted as the missing heir—the de Lancey children seemed to be innumerable—but he could no longer be regarded as a nonentity. His mother's name, by contrast, did him no good at all. Sir

Edmund Andros had been governor successively of New York, New England and Virginia but he would seem to have been unpopular—"as absolute as the Grand Turk" by one account—and left no other legend.

Captain Davenport sent for Richard on a day in late October when the *Romney* was still at anchor in the Upper Bay.

"You will realise, Mr Delancey, that New York is now the base for our squadron on the North American Station. This is our dockyard and source of supply. Lord Howe has therefore appointed Commodore Harvey to command here under his general direction. The commodore will need a small staff to assist him in his duties and I have been asked whether I can recommend a midshipman to serve under his broad pennant. Yours is the name I incline to forward but I thought it proper to ask you first whether you would welcome such an appointment."

"I am most grateful for your consideration, sir, and am happy to accept."

"The commodore's staff will comprise Lieutenant Huggins and, as secretary, Mr Greenway. Mr Huggins was formerly master of the *Chatham* and has useful experience in that branch of the service. The commodore is a senior captain who began his service, I believe, on the lower deck. You will be assistant secretary and aide-de-camp with social as well as clerical duties. You will live ashore and assist the commodore in his work, helping to maintain good relations with our American friends."

"Very good, sir."

Very much the aristocrat, Captain Davenport took snuff and looked keenly at Richard. After a moment's pause he went on to add a further word of explanation:

"In submitting your name to his Lordship I am influenced, in part, by your family connections. I have been given to understand that you are a cousin of the New York de Lanceys. Have you met them?"

"No, sir."

"I have no doubt that you will. Four of them are active in the king's service. James de Lancey, a wealthy landowner, is colonel of the Westchester Light Horse. Oliver de Lancey has raised three battalions of loyalist troops for the defence of Long Island, being given the local rank of brigadier-general. He has two sons, Stephen and Oliver. Stephen is a lawyer but is now lieutenant-colonel in his father's brigade. The younger Oliver is a professional soldier brought up in Europe and presently serving in the 17th Light Dragoons. From these facts you will readily understand that the de Lanceys are important members of the Loyalist or Tory Party in New York."

"Yes, sir."

"Very well, then. I expect that your appointment will be confirmed within the next few days."

Richard came away from this interview with mixed feelings. He looked forward to living ashore and exploring New York. He wanted to make himself known to his cousins. He had to realise, however, that he owed his appointment to his name. He guessed that the commodore and his lieutenant were useful men in the dockyard but unlikely to shine in society. His task would be to steer the commodore through American drawing-rooms, advising him on etiquette and suggesting what compliments he should pay and to whom. The fact was, however, that he himself knew nothing about high society and was ill qualified to advise anyone. It was also apparent that he had been a relative failure as a sea officer. This was why he could be dispensed with so far as the *Romney* was concerned. Another youngster would do as well and probably better. He was being sent back to his desk, with lessened chances of further promotion. Service ashore might count towards sea-time (although he was not sure about that) but it would do little to qualify him as lieutenant. In one way he could regard this appointment as a setback, a step in the wrong direction. On these lines he might never reach commissioned rank at all.

A week later Richard was allocated a "cabin" on the top floor of No. 48 Wall Street. The commodore, a weather-beaten and inarticulate old seaman, had his quarters on the first floor and his offices on the ground floor. The garden wall from which the street took its name, once the boundary of old Peter Stuyvesant's property, had mostly disappeared by this time, giving place to houses. One of these, No. 3, was the headquarters of the military commandant; another, No. 25, was the public Guard House. There was plenty of accommodation for military purposes because the rebel families had fled elsewhere. General Sir William Howe thus had his headquarters at 3 Broadway, Lord Howe at 10 Hanover Square and the 17th Light Dragoons had their barracks at 1 Bowery Lane. Richard quickly found his way round the town, discovering that Wall Street was very central to all his normal activities. It led in the one direction to the King's Wharf on the Hudson River, in the other direction to the various shipyards on the East River. Trinity Church, where his ancestor lay buried, was in Broadway, not far from the corner of Wall Street. John Street, where the theatre was, ran parallel, further north, and William Street led from Wall Street towards Hanover Square and, beyond that, to Fort George and City Hall. The commodore had plenty of business to transact and Richard was soon familiar with each headquarters and every contractor's office. He realised for the first time that the maintenance of any one man-of-war or transport was a big administrative task and that the supply of a squadron took fifty times as much thought and effort. Lord Howe's squadron was not formed for battle—at this stage of the war he had virtually no opponents—but its administration problems were still immense. There was much, therefore, to do on shore.

Richard found time, nevertheless, to attend the French Fencing and Dancing Academy in Little Dock Street. This academy had been opened the year before by proprietors who were improbably named Du Poke and De St Pry. The fashion of the moment was for the cotillon and for French country dances, accomplishments to be acquired on the first floor. Fencing was pursued on the floor below and was regarded as a school of manners as well as of arms. It cannot be said that Richard was a born dancer but he learnt the rudiments. He was no more than competent as a swordsman but, again, he came to know the basic rules. He soon felt qualified to play a part—a humble part—in New York society.

Successful as he might be in learning manners, Richard was far less successful in teaching the commodore or Lieutenant Huggins. Both were elderly and Huggins was lame, having been shot through the leg in 1761. Neither could bow gracefully or turn a compliment and neither had much inclination to learn. Richard could serve the commodore, however, by telling him in a loud whisper the names of the people he was to meet. "Dr Delany, Colonel Van Ruyven, Mr and Mrs Roosevelt, Major Livingston, the Rev. Hendrickson . . ." It was also his self-imposed duty to head the old seaman off his main topic of light conversation—the need for economy in the purchase and issue of naval stores. This was not a subject of absorbing interest among the ladies, and their husbands, many of them contractors, looked at it from a different point of view. It was better, on the whole, if the commodore said nothing at all. Richard also took it upon himself to answer questions about the current fashions in London. All the American ladies, and even the more foppish of the men, were apt to ask about the modes at court. When asked "What is being worn this season?" the commodore was completely at a loss. He had once been mate of a collier out of North Shields and he was still given to chewing tobacco in secret. So the fashions in velvet, silk and brocade were definitely not his speciality. Richard was equally ignorant, having never seen London in his life but only Woolwich and that mainly from the river. He had learnt a method, however, of answering this particular question. "What is being worn?" he would repeat, studying the fair questioner's own dress. "The better sort of folk are wearing sprigged muslin with white lace, the fan to match." He would then simulate a start of surprise and add "Pretty much what you are wearing, Ma'am, now I come to think of it." This sort of reply was well received and he gained the reputation of being a well-bred young man. On social occasions he wore a second-hand civilian suit, disguising his humble rank, and was introduced as "Mr Delancey, of the Royal Navy."

Moving in the fringes of New York society, Richard was bound to meet his American relatives sooner or later. The first of them he saw was Miss Charlotte de Lancey, aged sixteen, who made a brief appearance at his dancing class. She showed little interest in Richard, seeming distant and proud. She chattered in a corner with her constant companion, Miss Elizabeth Floyd, daughter of Colonel Floyd of Long Island. Being a year older, Richard attributed correctly her aloof manner to shyness but made no progress with her after their first introduction. All that he learnt from the girl was that her male relatives were mostly out of town. Her father, the brigadier-general, was with his brigade and so was her elder brother, Stephen. As for the younger Oliver, he travelled incessantly in search of recruits for the 17th and had not been home that fall. Charlotte deserted the dancing class after perhaps three sessions, either because she thought the other pupils socially inferior or because the journey was too tiring. Although not attracted by Charlotte, who was rather plain at this time, Richard was disappointed at her quitting the class and rather despaired of meeting his cousins. Mere midshipmen were probably beneath their notice, whether related or not.

The situation changed abruptly in November. General de Lancey's home was at Bloomingdale, seven miles out of town and close to the Hudson or North River, beyond which lay New Jersey, much of it in rebel hands. On a dark and cold night a party of the enemy crossed the river and raided Bloomingdale. Breaking into the house, they plundered the ground floor. When Mrs de Lancey came downstairs they abused and insulted her. They ill treated poor Charlotte and her friend, Miss Floyd, attempting to wrap both girls in a burning sheet. They finally set fire to the house. By then the two girls had escaped, Charlotte carrying her infant nephew (Stephen's child), and were hidden in a swamp. When rescued in the morning by Mr Charles Apthorpe, the half-frozen girls were unable to walk. When news of this outrage reached New York there was widespread indignation, many folk concluding that the rebels had been mad or drunk or both. The two immediate results of this affair were the family's moving into town and the general's return from Long Island. With Bloomingdale much damaged and plainly unsafe, Mrs de Lancey came to stay with her daughter-in-law at 30 Nassau Street and it was there that her husband joined her, vowing vengeance against the sort of cowardly riff-raff who made war only on women and children. It was at this juncture that Richard paid a formal call to inquire after Miss Charlotte's health. Having learnt that she was in bed but recovering from shock, he went on to offer his services as a poor substitute for her brothers. If the name could be discovered of the rebel leader responsible he proposed to call him out as a poltroon and a thief. It was no more than a polite gesture but the elderly general expressed his thanks.

"I'm vastly obliged, young man, and Mrs de Lancey will feel as I do when she hears of your sympathy. As for punishing this ruffian, I may well challenge him myself. I had little thought that the war would come to this sort of pointless and petty crime. I had supposed that this could have been a war between gentlemen."

Before he left the house Richard had been accepted as a relative.

"So you are my father's great-great-grandson—my cousin thrice removed. I never heard of my father's earlier marriage but there was time enough for it. Or was he married, eh? Never mind that, however, you are a de Lancey. Did you ever see our coat-of-arms?"

Richard was presently shown an achievement which read:

AZURE: a tilting lance proper, point upward with a pennon argent bearing a cross gules, fringed or, floating to the right, debruised of a fesse, or.

CREST: A sinister arm in armor embowed, the hand grasping a tilting lance, pennon attached, both proper.

"Come to think of it," said the general, "I have a note somewhere of the Andros arms. Have you considered, young man, that two of your ancestors—Etienne de Lancey and Sir Edmund Andros—must almost certainly have known each other?" Richard admitted the likelihood of this, thinking to himself that their mutual dislike had probably been instant and obvious. Of more immediate concern to him, however, was the fact that he himself had now, socially, arrived.

From the beginning of 1777 New York took on a new lease of life. The rebel cause seemed hopeless, especially after the capture of Newport, Rhode Island. Mr James Rivington, who had gone to England in 1776, was back again and had renamed his newspaper *The Royal Gazette*. Its columns had now to record a glittering social life, culminating in General Howe's investiture as Knight of the Bath. He and his staff—the affable and popular Colonel Pattison, the brilliant Major André—were to be seen on every public occasion. The Garrison Dramatic Club was active—for charity—at the Theatre Royal in John Street. The plays performed included *The Beaux Strategem* and a piece by Mr Sheridan called *The School for Scandal*. There were public concerts and often a military band playing on the walk near Trinity Church. Balls and dances were frequent, some given by Governor Tryon and others privately at Hick's Tavern. Then, as the weather improved and the days lengthened, there were outdoor activities. Horse races were held at Ascot Heath, Long Island. Then fox hunting gave place to cricket matches at Brooklyn or Greenwich. Brooklyn was also the scene of boxing and golf, with wonderful fish dinners to follow at the Ferry House. It had become the fashion to dine at four in the afternoon with blinds drawn and candles lit. Dinners were innumerable and there was no shortage of anything. Naval and army officers were invited everywhere and few were more popular than General Clinton, the son of a previous governor who had served in the New York Militia and could be counted as a New York man.

One who certainly enjoyed the fun was Richard Delancey, who could do so with a clear conscience. His shore appointment carried with it social responsibilities and he was often to be found

at the commodore's elbow on public occasions. He was also an
accepted member of the de Lancey family circle, sometimes
dining with cousin James, sometimes with the general, and as
frequently escorting Charlotte and her mother to Vauxhall
Gardens or the Play. He lacked the means to live in such expen-
sive society but his cousins were considerate and he was never
for long in debt. Charlotte's favourite reading was *Hoyle Improved
or New Maxims for Playing the Game of Whist* but Richard pro-
fessed ignorance of the game, knowing that he could not afford
to lose money at cards. His temptation was to accept presents
from navy contractors, some of whom imagined that he might
have some influence over the commodore. He had none, in fact,
but he came to realise that Lieutenant Huggins and Mr Greenway
were doing a profitable business on the side. They eventually
made him a small allowance on the pretext that he was doing
extra duty, their real purpose being to purchase his silence. He
had, in fact, no detailed knowledge of their transactions, nothing on which he could have based a report, and felt in no way
involved. He needed the allowance, however, and took it, being
afterwards better able to pay his way. It was as near as he
came to accepting a bribe and a great deal nearer than was proper
or even wise. But what was he to do? He could not do a flag
lieutenant's work on a midshipman's pay and his social activities
were all, he believed, in a worthy cause.

Looking back afterwards on the summer of 1777, on the parties and fireworks, on the picnics and plays, Richard had an
impression of unreality. In the foreground were the gaily coloured
uniforms and pretty frocks but in the background was a war in
which the professional soldiers should long since have routed
the amateurs. There had been no such result as yet but it was
not for want of talent on the British side. The generals were

experienced, skilful and resolute. They were popular, moreover, and had proved themselves in earlier campaigns. They were backed by men-of-war and supported by thousands of American loyalists. Their rebel opponents had begun the war with an attempted invasion of Canada, an operation which had been disastrous. Washington was now on the defensive and his forces were known to be ill-recruited and ill-supplied, lacking besides in cavalry and guns. There was something wrong, however, with King George's men, a reluctance to push their efforts to a logical conclusion. They were always negotiating when they might be expected to attack. They had been in winter quarters when the enemy had been on the move. Their movements, when they began to move, were based more on political than upon military considerations. As for the loyalists, with their over-officered weak battalions, they were ready to police their own immediate vicinity but were they ready to fight the other side? Some of the Tories were loyal enough but how many of them were thriving (as the de Lanceys had been) on military contracts? And how many of them were using the situation to settle their grievances and ruin their rivals? How many, for that matter, were acquiring the town property of men who were serving in the rebel army? Land values might rise dramatically some day in a town built on so restricted a site, hemmed in by deep water. Building lots now sold for a few hundred dollars—lots in Wall Street, John Street or Hanover Square —might be worth as many thousand by the end of the next century. To own as much as they did of New York would, quite possibly, make the de Lanceys a very wealthy family. That the Boston folk who began the rebellion were a seedy group of dishonest tradesmen was a matter of common knowledge, not seriously open to dispute. But were the loyalists so very much better? Richard began to have his doubts.

Richard's change of heart about the American colonies was hastened by that most loyal of officers, the old commodore himself. That officer's condemnation of the rebels was outspoken but he had almost as low an opinion of the Navy Board. Looking up one day from a letter just received, old Harvey fairly expressed his exasperation.

"Listen to this, Mr Huggins—harkee, Mr Delancey—I am told by the commissioners to charter a 250-ton merchantman from the firm of Oliphant, Rutgers & Son, the same to act as tender to the squadron. I am instructed by the same bunch of lubbers to have the *Phoenix* repaired at the Beekman & Peck shipyard. I am given to understand that blocks and cordage are best obtained from Mr Schuyler or from Mr McDougal. I am not to pay more than so much for mast-timber. My last payment for pitch was excessive and the warehouse rent comes to more than was paid during the last war. Is it I who am mad or have they taken leave of their senses?"

"You mean, sir," said Huggins, "that all rentals have gone up since George II's time?"

"Every child knows that!" shouted the commodore, "but what of the rest? What am I to make of this rubbish and who do they think I am?"

"It would seem, sir," said Huggins, "that they are a little out of touch."

"Out of touch, you say? Out of touch? They should long since have been in Bedlam. To begin with, Oliphant, Rutgers & Son are not in the shipping business and I doubt if they ever were. The Beekman & Peck yard is too small for the *Phoenix,* too small in fact for anything over 150 tons. Mr McDougal went bankrupt last year and Mr Schuyler is dead. As for mast-timbers and pitch, we had a good bargain and better than we shall have again. The fact is, Mr Huggins, that this way of doing business is nonsensical. No man alive can control what happens in New York from an office desk in London. His information is false or out-of-date, his notion is wrong of what is practicable and his instructions relate to some imagined situation which does not exist. I am vexed past the limits of endurance by this pettifogging correspondence. If I am *not* trusted I shall be happy to resign my charge to someone else. If I *am* trusted, why can't they have the good sense to leave me alone? Rather than pester me I could wish that some of these clerks would come out here and see the situation for themselves."

"I fear, sir," said Huggins, "that the Navy Board clerks are a slow-witted sort of people in the first place."

"They are no worse than the rest," growled the commodore. "The fault is not so much in them as in the system they are to maintain. A man on this side of the Atlantic cannot be directed by men whose offices are in London. Such a scheme does not accord with our only possible means of communication. Ministers may think to control what happens in Ireland—better though it might be if they left it alone—but America is too remote and should be left to those who know what the true position is."

Having thus conceded the case for American independence, the commodore pointedly asked Huggins and Delancey whether they had no work to transact. If there was in fact much to do— as he ventured to suppose—they had best do it rather than waste time in mere talk. Had that captured privateer *Nankee Doodle* been surveyed we should know by now whether she would serve as fleet tender. The necessary orders should go out this afternoon . . . at latest. Reflecting later on the commodore's words, Richard came to see the rebels' point of view. Old Harvey had endured for a few months what the American colonies had endured for over a century. What was his exasperation compared with theirs? Of course the Americans had been assisted against the French but the fall of Canada had left them with nothing to fear from that quarter. Now they wanted to control their own affairs and who could blame them? Thinking on these lines, Richard wondered how many others felt as he did? Was this the reason why the war progressed so slowly? He knew that some senior officers had flatly refused to serve in America. He had come to feel much as they did but was in no position to make the same gesture. Midshipmen were not supposed to have political opinions—nor opinions, for that matter, of any sort. No one cared whether they served or not. Richard had his own career to consider and would be wise, he knew, to keep his ideas to himself.

The scene which Richard was afterwards to remember most vividly was enacted in late October at the Merchants' Coffee House at the corner of Wall Street and Water Street. George Brewerton had just been promoted colonel in de Lancey's brigade and the occasion was being celebrated at a supper given by Oliver de Lancey (the general). There were only about one hundred and fifty men in the battalion that Brewerton was to command, as Richard happened to know, but that was no argument against holding a party. Those present, apart from the general, Stephen de Lancey and Brewerton, included several other officers of the same brigade, two or three more from the New York Militia, the tongue-tied Lieutenant Huggins of the Royal Navy, a merchant from Liverpool called Stanniforth (Stephen's partner in some trading venture), a lawyer from Albany called Yates and, last of all, Mr Midshipman Delancey. It appeared that the younger Oliver, who was in town, would be with them at a later hour. The company came together with much doffing of cloaks and clinking of spurs, swords being hung up near the door and a single midshipman's dirk adding a little to the martial display. With the exception of Huggins, it seemed doubtful to Richard whether anyone present had ever been under fire. The supper was excellent, however, the Negro servants were attentive, and all joined afterwards in the loyal toast, followed by a toast to Colonel Brewerton who replied modestly and briefly. Stephen then proposed "A speedy end to the rebellion." This led to a general discussion about the war, prolonged by the expert knowledge of all who were present.

"I have heard it argued in England," said Mr Stanniforth, "that our regiments here are at a sad disadvantage. In scarlet uniform, with parade-ground training, they are to confront men who are skilled in the backwoods."

"You may tell your friends, sir, that they are sadly misinformed." The general refilled his glass and passed the decanter before going on. "Our senior officers mostly fought here in the last war. They know the country better than the rebels can pretend to do, most of whom are townsmen and wearing a uniform almost as conspicuous in blue and white. On this point about wearing scarlet, you must know that there is a special uniform devised for colonial warfare. As for our fighting in too rigid formation, the rebels at Bunker's Hill were more governed by the manual than were the king's soldiers. No, sir, I have heard this said before but know it to be false. There are some true backwoodsmen on either side but there is little to choose between recruits from London and recruits from Boston."

"If we are at a disadvantage," said Stephen de Lancey, "it would arise more from control exercised over too great a distance. Orders from London can be outpaced by events."

"Very true, sir," echoed Mr Huggins before relapsing into

silence. There was further discussion and all agreed that the rebels had no monopoly in marksmanship or concealment.

"It is strange, for all that," said Mr Yates, "that we have heard nothing lately from the north. I had expected by now to have heard of General Burgoyne's approach. There has been fighting in that direction and there have been a number of conflicting rumours. Is there any recent news? I must confess that I have heard nothing."

There was nobody better informed and the resulting silence was broken tactfully by Colonel Brewerton, who proposed a toast to the Royal Navy. This was drunk with applause and all looked expectantly at Huggins, who in turn looked helplessly at Richard, who rose reluctantly to reply.

"General de Lancey, officers and guests. I rise to thank you all on behalf of the Royal Navy. We have been most hospitably entertained by our friends here in New York. We cannot claim to have destroyed the rebel fleet at sea because they don't seem to have a fleet [applause] but we have done something about the privateers of Providence. The result is that we are well supplied, as witness the table before us. Mr Leckie of Hanover Square has had his linen, Messrs Hugh and Alexander Wallace have had plenty of wine for us, Mr William Burton and Mr Michael Price have not been short of groceries and Mr Hugh Garvie has had the means of printing our invitation cards. The Royal Navy has had some part in protecting your sources of supply [applause] and you can depend upon us for future protection. It is the least we can do in return for your hospitality." Richard then proposed a toast to the New York Militia and Captain Bradford replied. One way and another it was a carnival evening. It came to be remembered, however, for another reason.

Captain Oliver de Lancey came in abruptly at about half past ten, threw his cloak and sword to a Negro servant and apologised to his father for being late. There was something about his brisk movements and decisive manner which marked him out as the professional, as the man who had recently been in battle. There was something else, though; a note in his voice which reduced the room to an uneasy silence.

"I am sorry to be the bearer of bad news, sir. General Burgoyne and his army have been forced to capitulate."

There was a moment of stunned silence and then, from the general, the inevitable question:

"But is this certain?"

"Quite certain, sir. Sir William Howe had Burgoyne's own dispatch and I have just come from his headquarters."

"I can still scarcely credit it. Do you know how it came about?"

"Burgoyne moved south in the expectation that he would meet another army coming north. He met only the enemy in superior numbers at a point where his communications were stretched beyond the limit."

"Where was that?"

"At Saratoga, sir."

"Good God! What now?"

"The likelihood is that France will enter the war against us. Once our forces have been turned about to face this new opponent we shall have none to spare for the reconquest of these American colonies. So far as this present war is concerned I should say, sir, that we have been defeated and that the colonies have gained their independence."

It was not, of course, as simple as that and those present were unwilling to admit defeat. New efforts would be launched, they said, new armies would be raised and new plans devised. After listening to all this talk Richard came to the conclusion that young Oliver—the only real soldier there—was obviously right. Unlike the rest he knew what he was talking about. He had also realised, as his father had not, that the family estates would all be forfeit and that the chief loyalists would all have to go into exile. Their period of wealth and influence was all but finished. In a few years they would be gone and in a few more years, forgotten. Nor could Richard share the grief that his cousins would soon be feeling. He did not believe that the rule of the colonies from London was really possible. It must break down, as Burgoyne's campaign had broken down, on the iron facts of distance and time. The party broke up early, the spirit having gone out of it, and Richard left with Oliver, the cousin he hardly knew. As they walked up the street they saw in the distance the brightness of fireworks lit at Ranelagh. Suddenly clairvoyant, Richard gestured in that direction and said:

"That's all finished, isn't it? That and the horse races at Brooklyn, that and the cricket matches and the masked ball. Our dream is over and we shall give way to sour-faced Bostonians. That's the truth, isn't it?"

"Yes, Richard, that's the truth. But I am luckier than the others. New York has never been my life. I belong, first and foremost, to the 17th Light Dragoons."

Chapter 5

CHARLOTTE

THE year 1778 found Richard still in New York and his contemporaries may well have thought him lacking in zeal for action. The circumstances which kept him to his desk were partly official, partly private. In the first place, old Harvey finally quarrelled with the Navy Board. His official correspondence, in which there had been a note of impatience from the beginning, became more vituperative as time went on. Following the dispatch of a final letter which was highly improper, and which Richard knew to be ill-considered at the time, he was relieved of his appointment. With him on the homeward voyage went his secretary, Mr Greenway. His successor was Commodore Edward Affleck, who made a rapid assessment of Mr Huggins, whom he replaced, and then asked Richard to stay. For his part, Richard came to realise that he had become essential to the commodore's office, having a knowledge of New York which no one else now possessed. Affleck was having difficulties with Howe's second in command, that "penurious reptile" James Gambier, and did not know one contractor from another. It was clearly Richard's duty to remain at least for the time being. This was what he told himself and even came to believe, but he had another motive and one quite apart from the interests of the service. He and Charlotte de Lancey had rather more affection for each other than their cousinship could entirely explain. When he first acted as her occasional escort she had not been particularly attractive. Girls of sixteen often pass through a plain phase and this had certainly been her fate. Apart from that, she was clearly an heiress, far above him in social position and quite beyond his aspirations. She was now eighteen and extremely pretty. Her parents had so far accepted Richard as a poor relative, assuming that Charlotte regarded him as almost a brother. As her future husband they already had someone else in mind: Nicholas Bayard (aged 26) whose family was of an importance comparable to theirs. Charlotte had no particular liking for him but the match was thought eminently suitable and that indeed it was.

So far in his life, and for years afterwards, Richard had assumed that marriage must wait until after he had reached the age of thirty. There was no certainty that he would have anything to offer even at that age; only the most remarkable good luck could make him an eligible suitor in the meanwhile. Recognising this, he had given little thought to girls. Nor had he much occasion to meet them socially before his arrival in New York. He had gained confidence since then, improved his manners and looked to his appearance. But the social customs of the time gave him little opportunity of meeting any young lady except as one of a group. Such opportunities as there were in the ballroom were limited and fleeting. A young man was expected to change partner at every dance and pay compliments to each partner in turn. To dance repeatedly with the same young lady was tantamount to announcing an engagement. All that happened, moreover, was under the eagle eye of mother, aunt or elder sister. There were ways, nevertheless, by which a preference could be shown and Richard was certainly Charlotte's favourite for a time and perhaps for as long as half a year. This halcyon period began with a stolen kiss at a ball given at Hick's Tavern by some officers of the 60th (Royal American) Regiment. There were, of course, more formal occasions, such as the Governor's Ball on the king's birthday, to which Richard was never invited, but he was present at other receptions as a de Lancey relative. The ballroom at Hick's Tavern opened on a small garden and it was here, on a moonlit summer night, that Charlotte was kissed. A minute later she had returned to the dance floor, remarking on her need for a breath of fresh air. Two minutes later she was dancing with Captain Mitchell of the New York Militia. There was no basis for scandal.

Unable to meet except very briefly, Richard and Charlotte began to correspond in secret, using as messenger one of the de Lancey servants, a young Negress called Susie. The letters were innocent enough but Susie came to realise that she was in a position to ask for more money than she had actually been paid. Charlotte, a spirited girl, boxed Susie's ears for insolence with the result that her most recent letter was delivered to her mother. Mrs de Lancey was naturally upset, fearing that some rumour would reach the Bayards and spoil all chance of the intended match. After lecturing Charlotte at length she told her husband of the letter and what its tone seemed to suggest. The result was a painful interview between the general and Richard, the former in resplendent regimentals, the latter in his uniform as a midshipman. In his character as an old campaigner, General de Lancey could not take too moral a line. As against that, he made it clear that there was to be no further social contact between Richard and Charlotte.

"There are some people, more especially in New England, who would come to the hasty conclusion that Miss de Lancey's reputation had been compromised. I do not think as poorly of her or of you. That she has been imprudent I must allow. That you have been ungrateful to your cousins here must be evident, even to you. But that is, I believe, the extent of the mischief. You are not to meet her again, young man, and I shall hope to advance the date of her engagement to Mr Bayard. She will forget her present or recent infatuation in a matter of weeks and my hope is that you will presently be stationed elsewhere."

"I owe you an apology, sir, for my seeming ingratitude. You and your family have shown me every kindness, more than a distant relationship would account for. I cannot thank you and Mrs de Lancey sufficiently for all that has made my life here so pleasant. I deeply regret that any error of mine should have resulted in any possible disadvantage to Miss de Lancey. My intentions, I assure you, were entirely honourable and I should presently have done myself the honour of asking for her hand in marriage."

"I am glad to hear that this was your intention, Mr Delancey, but you can hardly suppose that your proposal would have been welcome. In the first place, you are, I assume, as far as ever from holding commissioned rank?"

"That is true, sir, I must confess."

"May I ask then whether your father has sufficient interest to obtain your promotion at some future time?"

"He has no interest, sir."

"You have described him as a merchant. In what branch of commerce is he presently engaged?"

"He is a corn and forage chandler, sir."

"A corn and forage chandler . . . just so. That is something different from being—shall we say?—an East India merchant. You do not claim that he is in a large way of business?"

"No, sir."

"To how many servants does he offer employment?"

"An apprentice or two in the shop, sir, and one maid in the house."

"*One* maid . . . Now, as regards ancestry, you are well enough on either side. What you lack is present fortune or future prospects. It is my hope that you will prosper. You have the advantage of a good name. You have gained, since you came to New York, some of the manners and accomplishments which should make you welcome among people of refinement. On the other hand, your present appointment has given you no reputation in battle. You have done nothing to bring you to the favourable notice of your senior officers. I should have no reason to be proud of you as my son-in-law."

"I quite understand, General."

"These are times when we who wear the sword must be judged by our conduct in the presence of the enemy, not merely by our ability to make ourselves agreeable in the drawing-room. Your courage has still to be proved."

Richard had to admit the truth of this but raged inwardly against the brigadier-general's pose as a veteran of the wars. He owed his military rank to his gesture of raising three weak battalions, each far below its proper strength. He and his men had never faced the enemy or fired a shot. Richard's own service had been hardly more eventful but he was only eighteen years old. He now did his best to defend himself, thinking of Charlotte as the only girl he had ever loved, forgetting that she was almost the only girl he had ever met. He argued and pleaded but he knew inwardly that the general was right and that his cause was hopeless. It was a painful and humiliating interview and ended with Richard promising not to speak or write to Charlotte again. He knew that her engagement to Mr Bayard would now be hastened and that the general would take steps to ensure that he

himself would be posted elsewhere. It came as no surprise, therefore, when Commodore Affleck sent for him. He was an elderly
man, a fine officer and much more of a gentleman than his pre-
decessor had been. He began by thanking Richard for his useful
work, the burden of which had been increased by Mr Huggins's
removal, more especially as his successor had not yet arrived.
The commodore chose his words with care:

"Whether you know it or not, Mr Delancey, there are some
folk here, good friends of ours, who want to see you stationed
somewhere else. I do not propose to discuss their motives nor
do I blame you for the situation to which they indirectly refer.
We have all been young once. We have all made mistakes. We
have all had unreasonable aspirations at one time or another and
we all know what it is to burn our fingers." The commodore
looked again at a letter that lay before him and smiled slightly
before going on:

"In the ordinary way I should not allow myself to be influenced by private complaints—not without proof that some
regulation had been broken—but we are not in a position to
quarrel with such allies as we have. There are, moreover, two
other considerations and I shall take them in order. The first
concerns your future in the service. When I came here I needed
you—and Mr Huggins, of course—to advise me of local conditions, problems and pitfalls. I have to thank you for your good
work in this respect. But I am no longer a newcomer and feel
that you are no longer essential. It also seems to me that you
must gain more sea experience if you are to reach commissioned
rank. You have gained some useful knowledge ashore—this I
fully realise. You know something of naval administration
and official correspondence. You know something of what might
be called diplomacy. You would some day make a good flag

lieutenant. In the meanwhile, you need a period of practical sea-
manship. That is one consideration but there is also another."
There followed a pause during which the commodore looked at
Richard as if still trying to assess him by some other criterion.

"You have had an active social life while in New York, Mr
Delancey, and have lived rather beyond your means as a midshipman. Might I know whether you have had a generous
allowance from your father?"

"My father has been quite as generous, sir, as his means will
afford. My allowance from him has been no more, however, than
what is needed by a member of the gunroom mess."

"So I should have guessed. And you are not in debt?"

"No, sir."

"So . . . ?"

"I have relatives here in New York."

"I know. That is agreed. Well?"

"There are times when I have been in debt."

"But the debts have been paid. Well?"

"Really, sir . . ."

"Well, Mr Delancey?"

Richard was silent but the commodore continued to look at
him expectantly.

"I have had an allowance sir," said Richard finally, "from Mr
Huggins and, until he went, from Mr Greenway."

"Indeed? And why were they so generous?"

"They recognised, sir, that I was doing more than my share
of the work. It was I who attended Commodore Harvey ashore
because—"

"Because Mr Huggins is lame? Quite so. And you did much
of the correspondence as well. But was that the sole reason for
their generosity?"

"I don't know, sir. I never asked for anything."

"No, I don't suppose you did. But how did Huggins and Greenway come to have the money? Did they take it out of their pay?"

"I couldn't say, sir."

"Well, what if they didn't?"

"They were paid from some other source, sir."

"What other source?"

"I suppose, from the contractors."

"But you knew nothing of this?"

"No, sir."

"Or you preferred to know nothing."

"I was never told, sir."

"But you could have guessed."

"Yes, sir."

There was a long silence while the commodore considered him afresh.

"How old are you, Mr Delancey?"

"I am nearly nineteen, sir."

"With so much to learn . . . I must tell you, first of all, what I have decided. Then I shall give you a little advice, not as from a senior officer, but merely as from an older man. My decision is simple. You must leave this station but I shall take no further action. Nor—come to think of it—could I have done so in any case. I have no facts to lay before a court martial. I know what has been happening but have no proof of what I know. It is enough, for the moment, to have put a stop to it and that I have done. So far as you are concerned, the matter is closed. It remains to give you a piece of advice and it is this: a small dishonesty leads to a greater. In this matter of the supply contracts I do not suppose that Mr Huggins went to the various contractors and asked for the usual discount. It was they who came to him, asking how the usual payment should be made. He did not allow them to bid against each other. He did not, I think, advise our doing business with the wrong firm, accepting the higher tender or overlooking the poor quality of the supplies. That would have come later. All he did, and all Greenway did, was to follow the existing practice. You were still more innocent. You took your share but you never knew where the money came from. You were careful not to ask. You chose not to know. I understand already what your excuses are. You are young and inexperienced. You were doing more than your share of the work and meeting more of your share of the expense. You had made for yourself a certain position in society. Your clothes had to fit and your shirts had to be clean. Without something extra, you could not have done all that you were expected to do. All that is true but my acceptance of those undoubtful facts will not lead me to alter the advice I have to give: *Don't do it again.* It is not enough to be ignorant of dishonest practice. It is not wise to accept money from sources unknown and for services unspecified. It is improper and foolish to accept a reward for being ignorant. You are old enough and certainly intelligent enough to know that the money offered you *must* have been obtained dishonestly. You should now realise what your position would be if future supplies from the same firm are overpriced and rotten. 'What a pity,' you might be told, 'that we should have any disagreement after we have been such good friends. And what would be the result of certain information coming to the knowledge of your superior officers? Come, let's avoid any unpleasantness. We'll lower the price—a little. We'll replace the canvas—some of it. We'll improve your commission—doubling it. And we'll be more careful next time—to put the rubbish under the better-quality cordage.' I'll sum it up for you again: a small dishonesty leads to a greater and the last in the series leads to a court martial."

"Aye, aye, sir," said Richard, almost in tears. "And thank you, sir, for your advice. I'll do as you say—I will, sir, honestly."

"Very well then. Not a word of what has happened—not a word of what I've said—to anyone. I have obtained a midshipman's berth for you in the sloop *Falcon,* Captain Mottram. That ship is to sail shortly for the southern part of the station. Mottram has pointed out that French forces have already reached America and that French prisoners may fall into our hands. He wishes to have an officer who can speak French. He is glad to accept you and you will be rated as midshipman. I should add that he has a great reputation as a navigator and that one of his officers, I have been told, has a special interest in gunnery. You will thus be more in the way of learning your trade. It is my belief that you will do well and become a valuable officer and a credit to the service."

So ended Richard's service in New York. He had three days in which to say goodbye to his friends. Of his cousins he saw only young Oliver, the only one of the family, Charlotte excepted, whom he really admired. On his last evening he dined in mess with the officers of the 17th Light Dragoons, the only regular cavalry to serve in America at this time. Some of the officers were away on duty and it was only a small group which lingered finally over the port. All knew by now that, France having declared war, the situation had changed dramatically for the worse. Much to his surprise Richard was asked to give the others the naval point of view. He did so with some hesitation, disclaiming any knowledge that a senior officer would have had.

"All I have seen of the war has been as a midshipman on the

staff of the commodore, New York, whose concern is with the supply and repair of ships, both men-of-war and transports. From this dockyard point of view I have come to realise that our chief weakness lies in our growing shortage of mast-timber. Our larger ships are masted with timber from New Brunswick and Maine. We have had no other source of supply for the best part of a century."

"But what happened," asked Oliver, "before the American colonies gained their present importance? Did we use our own timber?"

"Only for small vessels, sir. Larger mast-timber came from the Baltic and always had. For a three-decked ship there was a special way of shaping three trees to make a single mast, a very skilled business as I understand. Trees from Maine are big enough to be used singly, producing a better mast with far less trouble. So we had come, you see, to rely on America."

"And the American supply vanished," asked Oliver, "when the colonies rebelled?"

"Yes, sir."

"So we must go back to the Baltic?"

"That trade ceased long ago and is not easy to revive, sir. As for making a mast from three separate tree trunks, the secret seems to have been lost. The carpenters who used to do it have long since died."

"What will be the result, then, of the shortage?"

"Well, sir, our ships will soon be in battle against the French. Some will be dismasted, perhaps, and must return to their base. It may then prove impossible to refit them for sea. We can then suffer defeat from lack of timber."

"And what will the French do when dismasted?"

"They can have new masts from their American friends for

as long as they have a dockyard in which to do the work."

There was silence for a minute or two, broken by the mess president circulating the decanters. It was Major Tarleton who asked the question which had occurred perhaps to everyone.

"Do the French know about this?"

"They are bound to find out, sir, aren't they?"

"How?"

"The Americans will tell them, sir."

"What then?"

"Well, sir, I should guess that the French will train their gunners to fire at our masts."

"But a mast," objected Woodcock, "is a slim target to aim at."

"Very true, sir," replied Richard. "They will train their gun-captains to aim carefully."

"Do we do that ourselves?"

"No, sir. We train them to fire rapidly at so short a range that they cannot miss. Our fire might be ineffective against an enemy who chose to engage at a greater distance."

"And we unable to mend the range after our masts and rigging had been damaged." It was Oliver who muttered this last conclusion, adding a moment later:

"It surprises me to hear all this from a midshipman, not from an admiral."

"Perhaps, sir, the admirals don't always tell us all they know."

"Maybe not, young man, but do other midshipmen know as much?"

"My recent service has been something which few youngsters undergo. For months past I have been in and out of the New York shipyards, seeing ships in dock, watching how they are masted, studying how they are repaired and listening to the ship-wrights, caulkers and riggers. These are men, sir, who know their trade. They talk about it among themselves and care nothing if a boy happens to be listening. Nothing I have told you is any proof of my cleverness. I am merely repeating what I have heard along the riverfront. It is common knowledge, sir, among the shipwrights."

"Have you reported this to the commodore?" asked Major Tarleton.

"No, sir."

"Why not?"

"He has not asked me for my opinion and I have learnt, as a midshipman, to avoid speaking out of turn."

There was a silence and the party presently broke up. Oliver, however, urged Richard to drink a final glass of port. "There is a little left in the decanter—a pity to waste it." Once they were by themselves Oliver thanked his cousin for his prediction of what might probably happen at sea.

"I need hardly tell you," he added, "that our armies are maintained by sea. Should the French control the coastal waters we should be starved into surrender. But there is something else you need to know, something I have myself been slow to grasp. Our present king succeeded to a throne which had been much weakened during the two previous reigns. He found that the country was ruled, for all practical purposes, by powerful lords who controlled Parliament and used it for their own ends. They had not ruled badly—indeed, they won the last war against France—but he could not see why he should be so powerless as compared with the French king. If the land was to be governed by wealthy landowners—why, he himself was the wealthiest landowner among them all. If they could appoint and influence members of Parliament, so could he. He called his men the King's Friends and set about regaining the influence his predecessors had lost.

He might have done it, too, but the American colonies chose this moment to rebel. He now had a war on his hands, a war which he might have won but which he is now almost certain to lose. You have told me what dangers threaten his fleet. You may not realise what disaster his troops may face."

"From American marksmen, sir, with French advisers?"

"We have worse enemies than those. In England there are men of wealth and influence who want the king to be defeated and who are doing all they can to make that certain. More than that, there are generals and admirals who will not serve or who will not fight whole-heartedly."

"But are there statesmen, sir, who are actually on the French side?"

"There are men who wanted to defeat King George in England but were glad to shift the whole conflict to America. Once he has lost the war he has lost his chance of a real kingship. Does General Howe want to beat the other side? I don't know. Nor do I know what is happening now. But our chances of victory in America are dwindling to nothing."

"And I suppose that the de Lancey estates will also dwindle to nothing, sir?"

"I should guess so, but not in time to help you with Charlotte. She will be married, depend on it, before the year's end. In the long run, for all that, our estates will be forfeit."

"Is there no chance of victory now, sir, none at all?"

"There is one chance. Remember, please, that what I tell you must go no further. Our only chance rests on some possible treachery on the American side, balancing all the treachery there has been on ours."

"But is that likely, sir?"

"It is not impossible. This is not yet a war simply between

Britain and France. It is still partly a war between the British themselves. We think of the rebels as Americans but they called themselves British until about three years ago. I am American but who is to tell the difference? General Washington held a local commission before all the trouble began. Had he been given the king's commission—and I am told that he applied for it—he would have been on our side, bound by his oath of allegiance. Well, there could be some other officer who might remember his former loyalty: especially if he felt ill-used by the rebel leaders or denied the promotion he deserved. We were all friends until quite recently and our present enemies include my relatives, my schoolfellows, my childhood neighbours. It was for many of us almost an accident which determined on what side we are on. Nor would it be very strange if a few of us were to change our minds. Some of our senior officers count on this happening and believe that it could change the whole course of the war."

"Could two or three deserters be as important as that, sir?"

"Not in themselves but any deserter could bring us vital information and his example would not be lost on his friends. You look doubtful?"

"Well, sir, I can see that this is a war of confused loyalties, but a man who changes sides after the war has begun has little, surely, to hope for. He will be distrusted in the army he has joined and will be hanged if captured by the army he has left."

"Such men may exist for all that. As an American I was asked if I knew of any officer who might come over to us. There was none I could name but I have talked to prisoners who were ashamed of the part they had played and who might have joined us had they not been captured first. Well now, we have finished the port and had best say goodbye. I hope we shall meet again, perhaps in London, and I shall expect to see you as a lieutenant."

On this note the conversation ended and Richard walked back to his quarters, where he had to pack his sea-chest and jettison all that he could not expect to take with him to his new ship. Among a litter of invitation cards and theatre programmes, he came across a poem he had begun to write and a watercolour he had attempted, Charlotte being the subject of each. Was he really broken-hearted? Well, nothing had affected his appetite or sleep. The truth was, he told himself, that she was much like any other girl of her class, pretty, stupid and spoilt. In a few days, in a few weeks at most, he would forget that she ever existed. In this belief, however, he was wrong. He was to remember her, in fact, until the day he died. There would be prettier girls and there would be more lingering kisses but it could be said of empty-headed Charlotte that she had been the first.

Chapter 6

CHARLESTON BESIEGED

THE *Falcon* (18) lay out in the East River and Richard, coming off from the shore, presented himself to Mr Bancroft, the first lieutenant, whose manner was far from encouraging.

"Well, youngster, I've heard something about you. On the commodore's staff they tell me. It seems to me that you've been too long ashore, too much of an idler, too seldom on deck and very rarely aloft. We shall have to change all that and see whether we can't make a seaman of you after all."

This marked the beginning of what was to be a difficult period in Richard's life. What the lieutenant said was all too true. He was fairly senior in years of service but knew too little of practical seamanship. The word had been passed that he was a mere quill-driver and that he was to be treated accordingly. Up to a point he was equal to the work that came his way, being good at boat-handling, average in navigation and fairly active aloft. He could never at this stage, however, have passed his lieutenant's examination in ship-handling. He had some rough treatment at Mr Bancroft's hands, being mast-headed for his worst mistakes and loudly cursed for minor instances of apparent neglect. He never, however, made the mistake of referring to his recent work ashore. He offered to fight any other youngster who sneered at him and was soon accepted as a member of the gunroom mess. There was a master's mate called Branning, two midshipmen called Hyatt and Tenison, the captain's clerk called

Priestman and a young volunteer (first class) called Mattingley.
All were on good terms and Richard found a special friend in
Mike Tenison, an Irish youngster from Roscommon, whose eye
he blacked on their first meeting. In the end, Richard learnt more
from his messmates than he did from Mr Bancroft.

Soon after the *Falcon* sailed on 14 October 1779, Richard was
bidden to dine at the captain's table where he also became
acquainted with the other lieutenant, Mr Maxwell. His first meeting with Captain Mottram had been brief and formal and this
was Richard's chance to make a good impression. He had little
help in this from Mr Bancroft, who was also present and who
referred, indirectly, to his lack of recent experience at sea. There
could be no defence against this sort of accusation but Richard
was rescued by Mr Maxwell, who asked him about the quality
of the work done in the New York shipyards. To this sort of
question he could give an intelligent answer, praising the work
done but casting a little doubt on the shipwrights' honesty.

"Our own are no better," said Maxwell sadly, "in fact they are
probably worse." A more general conversation followed and Captain Mottram questioned Richard about his fluency in French.

"I am fluent, sir," replied Richard, "but with a Guernsey
accent. I avoid using words which are peculiar to Guernsey but
I would never pass as a Parisian. I suspect that Guernsey French
is old-fashioned and that it may resemble, in that respect, the
French that is spoken in Quebec."

"You are probably right there," said the captain. "French
Canadians speak a sort of French heard in the last century, I
have been told."

"You might agree, sir," said Maxwell, "that Americans do
much the same. They use expressions like "gotten" which would
have been good English in 1600."

"It would not be wrong now," objected Mr Bancroft.

"It could be impolite, however," rejoined the captain amidst laughter. "But what about the American accent? You are partly an American, Delancey, but I should not guess it from your speech."

"I am a Guernseyman, sir, by birth and American only in having relatives in New York, people of my own name. But there are Americans in our forces, I have been told, whose accent suggests their origin. I have heard that said of General Clinton."

"I have met the general," said the captain, "and it is true. But the more manifest American accent comes from New England, from Boston. People in the southern colonies, where we are going, speak differently again and perhaps more pleasantly."

The dinner party did not end before Richard had managed to reveal, to Mr Maxwell, his own interest in gunnery. The response was immediate and he was offered the loan of a recent book on the subject, published in France. "I fear," said Mr Maxwell, "that the French have paid more attention to the subject than we have."

"They are well versed in the theory," admitted Mr Bancroft, "but it is another thing to handle the guns in half a gale with decks awash and big seas breaking over the forecastle. Seamanship matters more than the neat engravings made to illustrate a work on ballistics."

Captain Mottram intervened firmly at this point to say that theory and practice must go together. From his tone Richard concluded that disagreements on this subject had been frequent between the two lieutenants. He himself had much to learn from both of them and as much again from the captain. This voyage was his chance to learn and he realised that his teachers were among the best. And while all his sympathies were with the more civilised Mr Maxwell, his future depended, he knew, on gaining the good opinion of the more caustic Mr Bancroft. He would do this, he resolved, or die in the attempt.

There were moments during the voyage when death did not seem unlikely. He all but fell from the fore-topmast yard on one occasion, being saved only by the seaman nearest him. He came near to serious accident when reefing the fore-topsail in pitch darkness. His perseverance was rewarded in the end, however, when Mr Bancroft admitted rather grudgingly that his time in making sail had been fairly good; or better, anyway, than the time achieved by the other watch. Any trace of self-satisfaction was wiped out immediately and he was in disgrace again before the watch ended, but he had at least glimpsed the promised land (or sea) of his superior officer's approval. Harsh comments on his work had one useful result in making the seamen take his side. He was to learn much from the petty officers and was given many a useful hint by the captain of the foretop. He would never be as quick as the tongue-tied Branning but he was quicker than Hyatt and more thorough, at times, than Tenison. On the day when a seaman fell overboard and was rescued by a very cred-itable piece of boat-work, Richard received a brief compliment from the captain himself. He had become, he felt, a useful mem-ber of a very effective team.

By the accepted discipline of the period Captain Mottram was under no compulsion to reveal the object of the voyage to his officers, still less to his midshipmen. He did so, however, after the sloop had been at sea for two weeks, calling them together in the wardroom.

"Before we sailed, gentlemen, you must have been aware that a conjunct expedition was to take place. Merchant ships had already been chartered and some were being fitted for the transport of horses. It may be doubted, however, whether all the necessary tonnage will be ready before December. The destination of the expedition has been a secret but one I can now reveal to those who are to take part in the campaign. You must know, gentlemen, that Vice-Admiral Arbuthnot and General Sir Henry Clinton have agreed on a bold stroke: the capture of Charleston, the chief port of South Carolina, held at present by a rebel garrison. A strong force has been assembled with artillery sufficient to breach the defences. We already hold another port further south, Savannah in Georgia, where we have a more than sufficient garrison. In order to field the largest possible force against Charleston, Sir Henry plans to withdraw troops from Savannah for that service. I have been entrusted with his orders to the Savannah garrison commander. Having delivered them, I am to sail for Charleston where I am to join the vice-admiral's flag. We may have an active part to play in the siege and the more so in that the harbour at Charleston is too shallow for ships of any great tonnage. However, our immediate duty takes us to Savannah where we should drop anchor in three days, and where much will depend upon our discipline and good behaviour. This is not a war against an enemy country, against foreigners like the French or Spanish. These colonies are British and those to the south are thought to be very much on our side. At Savannah we are to consider ourselves among friends and must behave accordingly. On the other hand, we must not be more than friendly where the ladies of Georgia are concerned; nor, when Charleston falls, must we be other than civil towards the ladies of South Carolina. We need the good opinion of these people and we shall have to earn it. Please make this clear to seamen and marines alike. I say nothing at this stage about the dire consequences of misconduct in this respect. I would rather leave it to the good sense of the men themselves. Any questions?"

"Might I ask, sir," inquired Mr Bancroft, "whether the southern soldiers may not be lukewarm in the rebel cause?"

"Perhaps they are," replied the captain, "but don't count on it. I understand that the garrison of Charleston has been stiffened by men detached from New England, gunners and engineer officers especially and perhaps some Frenchmen as well. I should guess that the place will have to be bombarded and stormed."

"Should I be right, sir, in supposing that these southern colonies become impossibly hot in summer?"

"That is so, Mr Maxwell. We need to do our business before June, after which the fighting will cease by what amounts to mutual agreement."

There were no other questions but there was much discussion afterwards about how Charleston was to be captured. Mr Maxwell took the three midshipmen to his cabin and showed them the chart.

"The key to the position," he explained, "is this fort here on Sullivan's Island. Charleston has been attacked before, you see, in 1776 and Sir Henry was beaten off by the guns of what has since been named Fort Moultrie after the colonel who then commanded the South Carolina Militia. Now Clinton is to try again and I'll wager he won't make the same mistake again. He'll assault from the other side, you can be sure, but that fort will hold out against him. With the bar at the harbour mouth, the squadron cannot easily close the range. Frigates could enter, maybe, but their guns are not heavy enough to silence that fort. A sloop like this might pass the bar without much difficulty but would be blown out of the water. With Fort Moultrie fallen today, Charleston itself would fall tomorrow."

Falcon reached Savannah on 29 November 1779 to find the

place partly in ruins. It had been attacked in October by the
French Admiral D'Estaing and rebel troops commanded by General Lincoln. D'Estaing had been anxious to sail again and
persuaded Lincoln to make a premature assault. This had been
beaten off by Major-General Augustus Prevost whose men had
some reason to be proud of themselves. They were not, however, ready to embark nor was Mottram in any hurry to leave
while a French squadron remained (for all he knew) in the vicinity. He was still at Savannah for Christmas, sailing finally with a
convoy of transports laden with troops, artillery and horses.
Charleston was reached on 11 February and it soon appeared
that Sir Henry Clinton's army was already ashore and had captured James's Island. Frigates had crossed the bar in March but
the squadron was still faced by the guns of Fort Moultrie. A long
siege was in prospect and with no certainty of final victory. At
anchor in Five Fathom Hole, the *Falcon* did little more than provide occasional working parties for service ashore. It was while
commanding such a party that Delancey met some troopers of
the 17th Light Dragoons on James's Island. They belonged to a
single troop sent to stiffen the locally raised horse units, the regiment as a whole being elsewhere but he had news, at least, of
Oliver de Lancey. His more regular task was to visit the light-
house, making sure that the rebels were not using it as an
observation post. It could as easily have been occupied but the
decision had been taken to patrol it daily at different hours and
also occasionally at night. On this errand, after dark, Delancey
became aware of another boat approaching the island. The
sounds came from the creek on the landward side and Delancey
quietly ordered his five men to cock their muskets and spread
out to face the intruders. Drawing and cocking his own pistol,
he realised that this might be his baptism of fire. He had seen a

riot in Liverpool but he had not so far faced the enemy, least of all at the head of his own detachment. Was he destined to perish before his career had fairly begun? He became aware of his heart beating and realised that there was sweat on his brow. Men had landed from the boat and were moving quietly towards him. He waited until he could glimpse the leader's head against the sky, and then called out:

"Halt! Who's there?"

The man stood still and replied:

"I've a message for General Clinton."

"Are you armed?" asked Delancey.

"Yessir, I'll say."

"Drop your arms on the ground."

"Sure." There was the sound of a musket falling on the path.

"Step forward slowly but tell the others to stay where they are."

The man advanced with his hands above his head and Delancey told a seaman to search him while he himself kept the stranger covered.

"He is unarmed, sir," reported the sailor.

"Very well, then. Two paces forward and tell me who you are."

"I'm Philip Dobbs of Wapoo Creek."

"How many are there in your party?"

"One other man and a boy; Saul, my nephew."

"What do you want?"

"Like I said, I've a message for the general."

"From whom?"

"That I'm not saying."

"Are your men armed?"

"Isaac is. Saul ain't."

"Tell Isaac to ground his arms and come forward."

Philip was a middle-aged man with a straggling beard but

the white-haired Isaac seemed to be about eighty and Saul, when told to come forward, appeared to be about fifteen.

Making a swift decision, Delancey sent a seaman to collect the two fowling pieces and then marched the three colonists back to his own boat. On board the sloop again, he reported to Mr Maxwell, who reported in turn to Captain Mottram. Delancey was not a witness to the discussion which followed but he presently saw the three civilians being ushered into the launch, which moved off, under Mr Bancroft's command, in the direction of Stour Ferry. Mr Maxwell commended Delancey for his part in the affair, adding that the Americans were being taken under escort to Sir Henry Clinton's headquarters.

"This could be a good night's work, Delancey. Someone on the rebel side is trying to get in touch with us. Let's hope that the eleventh-hour loyalist is sufficiently high in rank."

Delancey was no party to the negotiations which followed. All he did, finally, was to take Philip Dobbs back to his boat and this after dark on the following night.

The siege of Charleston began on 1 April 1780, the first parallel being completed in two days and the siege works progressed inexorably according to the accepted rules of warfare. To ensure the success of the final bombardment and assault it was essential to move the ships of the line into position opposite the town. They were lightened sufficiently to cross the bar but Fort Moultrie still flanked the channel through which the ships would have to pass. When the orders came to sail in on 8 April the risk was all too obvious. Vice-Admiral Arbuthnot took the precaution, however, of sending in the *Falcon* ahead of the squadron and Delancey was detailed, on this occasion, to act as aide to Captain Mottram. So this, he thought, is to be my real baptism of fire. Against the stone-faced bastions of the fort the sloop's cannon could achieve nothing, while she would herself be a per-fect target for the far heavier guns which the fort would mount. The *Falcon* was a mere pawn, used to draw the enemy's fire and establish whether the heavier ships dared run the gauntlet. Delancey wondered whether the rebels would let the sloop pass, reserving their fire for the ships of the line. It seemed at first that this was their plan for the *Falcon* passed slowly before silent batteries.

"Incredible!" exclaimed the captain as he used his telescope. "There is activity round the rebel cannon but not a shot fired! What sort of game are they playing?"

Nor did the ships of the line face a more hostile reception. They passed the batteries in their turn, only the third of them being engaged by a single gun which was only belatedly joined by a second. The whole squadron moved to an anchorage in the upper harbour, sealing the fate of Charleston, the surrender of which was now inevitable. The *Falcon*, heading the line at first, dropped modestly astern after the fort was passed, anchoring further downstream as befitted a mere sloop. Perhaps for this reason it was to her that a boat from the shore directed its course after dark. Delancey, standing watch with Mr Maxwell, at once recognised his old acquaintances, Philip, Isaac and Saul, but they were accompanied this time by a fourth character who gave his name as Major Samuel P. Travell, officer in the rebel artillery, and a recruit, it seemed, to the service of King George III. Given leave to come on board, he reported himself to the officer of the watch, adding:

"Well, I gave you safe passage as I promised!"

"But how did you do it, sir?"

"I poured molten lead into the touch-holes. It took half an hour to clear them and that half-hour was enough."

"You commanded at the fort, then?"

"That is so. I thought it wise to quit before too many questions were asked."

"I can understand that, Major."

"As from tomorrow you can call me lieutenant-colonel."

Captain Mottram was informed presently of Travell being given that higher rank in the king's army but no news of Travell's appointment to an actual unit. He was to remain a passenger on board the *Falcon* and there was no plan, seemingly, for his employment. It soon appeared, moreover, that the fact of his treachery had become common knowledge.

On 5 May a boat came from the shore in broad daylight with several ladies aboard. They were received by Captain Mottram on the quarterdeck where the oldest of them, a formidable lady, explained the purpose of her visit.

"I am Mrs Esther Hoskins, widow of Colonel Hoskins of the South Carolina Militia. I live at the Galilee Plantation where these other ladies are neighbours of mine and well known to me."

Captain Mottram bowed but did not reply.

"My son, Captain Luke Hoskins, is serving with his company in the defence of Charleston. Two of these ladies have sons who are similarly employed and one of them, Martha Babcock, has a favourite nephew there who holds the rank of ensign."

Mottram repeated his bow with bare civility.

"We ask Sir Henry Clinton's permission to enter the town and take leave of our kinsfolk. We are aware, of course, that the town will be stormed in a few days' time."

"What makes you so certain of that?"

"Certain? Of course I'm certain. Everyone knows about it. It is the common topic of conversation. And what else is Sir Henry to do?"

Mottram declined any further discussion of Clinton's plans but agreed to send the ladies on to the general's headquarters where they could apply to him in person. He was issuing the necessary orders when Travell chanced to come on deck without the least idea of the ladies' presence. The scene which followed was highly embarrassing and Delancey, for one, could have wished that he had been somewhere else. Catching sight of Travell Mrs Hoskins drew herself up to her full height and pointed at him with her parasol.

"Really, Captain Mottram. I wonder to see Major Travell here as your guest! What name do we give to an officer who is traitor to his neighbours and former friends—who betrays the town which he is to defend—who is guilty of treachery towards his brother officers and enlisted men—who bites the hand that feeds him—who consorts with the enemy—who is utterly faithless and completely worthless, despised by every true American and spat upon by every patriot—who will go down in history as the lowest of the low? What do we call him, ladies? I call him Judas Iscariot!"

"Judas!" shrilled the other ladies and they were advancing on poor Travell in menacing fashion when Captain Mottram intervened.

"Ladies! If you will kindly proceed to the boat alongside you will be taken to Sir Henry Clinton's headquarters, where I am sure that you will be treated with every politeness. I must ask you to be as polite to my other guest and to remember that you are all guilty of treason, being in rebellion against our noble sovereign, King George, in whose territory you were born and to whom you owe a subject's loyal obedience. Good day to you, ladies!"

The painful scene ended, Travell going below without a word

and other people all busying themselves with their several tasks. As one of those present Delancey felt some sympathy with all concerned. Is the rebel to be praised who returns to his allegiance? Or is he guilty of a second treachery who goes back on his first? If Travell had gained promotion it was a step in rank, he thought, that had been dearly purchased.

The ladies had been right, of course, about Clinton's plans. His stranglehold on Charleston had been tightened and no relief was possible. His artillery had come closer to the target area and the defending ramparts had begun to crumble. Finally, on the night of 9 May, the final bombardment began, evidently the prelude to the final assault. Continuing all night, it brought General Lincoln to the point of surrender. From the deck of the *Falcon* lying quietly at anchor, Delancey and the other midshipmen listened to the thunder of the artillery and watched the whole sky lit up by flashes from perhaps a hundred gun muzzles. From the town itself came the red glare of burning and the crackle of the flames.

"A pity we have no share in this," said Hyatt.

"But what difference could we make?" asked young Tenison.

"I don't mean the *Falcon*," explained Hyatt, "I mean the navy. The admiral could have joined in the bombardment, couldn't he?"

"He and the general are not the best of friends," said Branning, and the others had to agree.

"That's often the way of it," said Hyatt. "Sailors and soldiers seldom see eye to eye."

"But they sometimes do," objected Delancey. "I'm told that Sir Henry thinks the world of Captain Elphinstone."

"And he could be right at that," concluded Branning. "But look over *there!*"

Shells were bursting now over the town and the noise had become more deafening than ever. It was this bombardment that was Delancey's introduction to war. While not himself under fire, he had begun to see what war must mean. It had, he thought, a rather frightening sort of attraction.

Delancey was not present to witness General Lincoln's formal surrender of the town but he was allowed on shore soon afterwards, he and Hyatt going together to see the damage done by the bombardment. They did not expect to see many houses intact. They found, on the contrary, that the town—as apart from the ramparts and gun emplacements—had suffered very little.

"After that cannonade," said Hyatt, "I expected to see total destruction."

"I think the gunners were under orders about that," said Delancey. "The general wanted the town for his own use afterwards. This is where he means to billet his troops."

"And the shops are reopening for the benefit of those new customers," observed Hyatt. "Are the people really friendly towards us, do you think?"

"They will be so long as we are here in force. One or two of the girls have looked at us with interest."

"You noticed that? There are some angry looks, however, from some of the older folk. They have some chimney-stacks to repair, some tiles to replace. Those who stayed in their cellars should have come to no harm, though."

"Anyway, it's good to be ashore."

"We are luckier in that respect than Colonel Travell. Were he to land he would be dead within the hour. Do you think he will be given a command?"

"No," replied Delancey after a little pause. "Were he to be

taken prisoner, you see, he would be hanged by the rebels. The general would not want that to happen. Travell might have a staff appointment in New York but would our senior officers trust him?"

"Having changed sides twice, you mean, they might expect him to change sides again?"

"I think they might have their doubts."

Sir Henry Clinton sailed for New York on 8 June, leaving Lord Cornwallis to complete the conquest of South Carolina. Travell, however, was left on board the *Falcon*, idle and depressed. He was tall, thin, dark-haired and dark in complexion, with a rather melancholy air but with an occasional flash of vivacity. Mottram regularly invited him to dinner and Delancey was present on one such occasion towards the end of June. Over the dessert Bancroft asked Travell whether he was a native of the southern colonies.

"No, sir. I come from Philadelphia and all my active service has been in the north. It was there, as one of the rebel officers, that I came to realise that we had lost the war."

"But, surely, Colonel," Maxwell protested, "the rebels, your former friends, have French help now. We have taken Charleston, to be sure, but Lincoln had come near to taking Savannah. King Louis has given them great encouragement."

"But look at the difficulties General Washington has to face! The continental currency is practically worthless. His supply system has broken down, so much so that the quartermaster general has resigned. The troops can neither be supplied nor paid. Their numbers are dwindling, recruits are few and some units may well mutiny. It is a miracle that the army exists at all. Its morale has never been lower."

"You were fighting, you thought, in a hopeless cause?"

"I was fighting, sir, in a war that should never have taken place. It could have been avoided with only a little patience on either side. I must confess, however, that I did not reach this conclusion unaided. I have had the honour of serving with a more senior officer who is—as I believe—the best soldier now serving on either side. He had come to the conclusion that a British victory would be in the best interests of the colonists themselves."

"And did he think that such a victory is likely?" asked Captain Mottram.

"He knew that he could bring it about, provided that General Clinton would follow his advice."

"He must be a remarkable man." Bancroft's tone expressed disbelief but Travell replied with emphasis:

"He is the greatest man I have ever met, possessing untiring energy, exceptional courage, quickness of decision and instant grasp of any situation. He has an instinct for war which amounts to genius."

"Has he no human weakness?" asked Maxwell wonderingly.

"He has a weakness for money, a love of luxury, a passion for thoroughbred horses and too great an interest in the other sex. These faults do not affect his brilliance as a commander in the field."

"You say, sir, that this officer's advice would bring us victory?" asked Mottram. "Do you know what his advice would be?"

"Yes, sir, I do. He would advise against the dispersal of our troops between north and south. He would urge a concentration of all our forces against Washington, securing all points at which the Hudson can be crossed. The rebel supplies of bread come from the country east of that river, their supplies of meat come from the west. Hold the line of the Hudson and Washington must either fight or surrender."

"But if he fought, sir, could he not still win?"

"Not if my friend's advice were followed in another particular. He suggests that the British should offer to recruit all of Washington's men, honouring all arrears of pay, undertaking to give them twenty guineas down with half-pay for seven years after the war has ended, offering a hundred acres of land to each private soldier and ten thousand acres to every general. In America, he says, money will go further than arms."

There was a shocked silence as Travell finished speaking, broken when Bancroft asked whether this plan would not involve a colossal expense. Travell replied promptly: "Do you think the present campaign is cheap, supported as it is by supply lines across the Atlantic? What does it cost to keep our armies in the field? What must we allow for keeping our ships in commission? We pay millions to fight Washington's men. The officer to whom I refer maintains that it would be cheaper to buy them. I think myself that this is the fact."

"On this principle," objected Maxwell, "we should be using American troops to fight our battles."

"We are doing that already," replied Travell, "and they have British deserters on the rebel side as their opponents!"

"Such a situation," exclaimed Mottram, "as a novelist would hardly dare invent!"

"But what is so strange about it, sir?" asked Travell. "We were all British until about five years ago. Have our natures so changed in the meanwhile? This war has been senseless from the beginning. It is time that the killing gave place to a quiet discussion among men who should be neighbours and friends as well as relatives."

"May I assume, sir, that this officer of distinction is about to resume his allegiance to the king as you have done?" asked Mottram.

"He should have done so already," was Travell's reply. "He and I were to come over at about the same time. The silencing of Fort Moultrie was his idea and he arranged my transfer so as to make it possible. I should not have revealed as much as I have had I not assumed that he was now in our camp."

"Gentlemen," said Mottram gravely, "what we have just heard from Colonel Travell is of the greatest importance. We must repeat no word of it until the colonel tells us that the matter is no longer secret."

"We are all grateful, sir, to the colonel for taking us into his confidence," said Maxwell, "and he has given us much to think about. One thing I have learnt is that, in war, you learn all about your own difficulties and conclude too readily that your opponents have no troubles of their own. It is easy, in fact, to give up at the moment when your enemies are on the point of collapse."

"Very true, Mr Maxwell," said Mottram, "and this must be a lesson for all of us."

The conversation became more general and Travell was heard to remark that time was heavy on his hands. He had thought to spend his idle hours in learning French but he had no books in that language to study. Afterwards, when the party was breaking up, Delancey went up to him and asked, with some hesitation, whether he could be of help. "I am fluent in French, sir, but with a provincial accent." Travell accepted this offer and lessons in oral French led to something like a friendship or as much of a friendship as can exist between a youth and a much older man. Soon after *Falcon* sailed, on 14 July, Delancey

expressed his hope that Colonel Travell would be given a command or at least a staff appointment. Travell, who was evidently
depressed, said that he had little hope of it.

"You see the difficulty, youngster. Clinton will never trust me.
But, apart from that, how can he appoint a recent recruit, recently
an enemy, to any post which anyone else could possibly want?
How should he prefer me to an officer who has served loyally
since the war began? And how would my appointment be
received by officers who were to serve under me?"

"You told us, sir, of a more senior officer who may by now
have returned to his original allegiance. Were he received with
respect, your own position would be greatly improved, would it
not?"

"I counted on that but am no longer so sure. That friend of
mine is lucky in that his recent marriage has brought him some
Tory friends. The young lady to whom I am engaged has no such
connections and may well think poorly of me for quitting the
rebel army. She should have received my letter before now. For
all I know, her next letter to me may be the last I have from her.
She may judge me harshly but what else could I have done?
Which way was I to turn, and what should I do now? And when,
to begin with, should we reach New York?"

"In about the third week of August, sir, if the present wind
holds."

"I almost dread the day, glad as I shall be to see the end of
this voyage."

The *Falcon* reached New York on 18 August and dropped
anchor in the East River. There had been no recent fighting in
the vicinity, the rebels having been beaten off in an attack
on Staten Island some months before. The town looked as pros-
perous as ever, and Delancey looked forward to going ashore.

In this, however, he was doomed to disappointment. Captain Mottram, sending for him, explained that Vice-Admiral Arbuthnot's orders were that he should remain for the present on board the sloop and that he would be sent back to England when opportunity offered. His disappointment in this was more than matched by that of his friend. Travell was equally ordered to stay in the ship, being told indirectly that this order was for his own safety. Were he to land the probability was that he would at once be challenged to a duel by some American hothead who had heard about the events which led up to the fall of Charleston. It was thought possible that he might be posted to the West Indies but no actual appointment had been made. There was no news of any important desertion from the rebel army. To make matters worse, moreover, Travell received a number of cruel letters from complete strangers. People, who could accept his changing sides, could never, it seemed, forgive his betrayal of Fort Moultrie. Travell showed none of these letters to Delancey but it was easy to guess their contents from his angry or sad reaction. It was as easy to guess that he had received no letter from the lady to whom he was engaged. He could now obtain French books from the town but it is doubtful whether he did more than glance at them. He was a man whose career was apparently finished. For his own part, Delancey was in almost equal despair about a career which had scarcely begun. He had, however, the advantage of youth and could resume, with Maxwell's help, his studies in navigation. He might not achieve promotion but he could at least try to deserve it.

Chapter 7

THE TURNCOAT

WHEN Captain Mottram sent for Delancey one day in autumn it seemed for a moment that his detention on board the sloop was to end. That was not the purpose of the admiral but he was given, instead, a temporary attachment which would provide him at least with a change of scene. Captain Mottram vowed him to secrecy and told him that he was to serve for a short time on board the sloop *Vulture* (18 guns). "Captain Sutherland has recently asked for a French interpreter and has now accepted my assurance that you would prove suitable. That ship is to proceed on a secret mission, the details of which are known to very few. You may remember an occasion when Colonel Travell, dining as my guest, told us of a more senior officer of the rebel army who might be expected to return to his allegiance?"

"Yes, sir."

"He did not tell us that officer's name but he evidently supposed that he would come over to our side in the immediate future. The time for this move on his part has, seemingly, arrived. Our object is to ensure his safe passage from the rebel lines to ours. If you recall what Colonel Travell said about this officer's known abilities you will understand what importance must attach to this operation."

"Yes, indeed, sir."

"The sloop *Vulture* is to take on board an officer from Sir

Henry Clinton's staff, Major André, Sir Henry's adjutant-general. You will probably have heard of him."

"I have met him, sir."

"Of course you will have done. He is much in New York society and extremely popular. He is also much in Sir Henry's confidence. His orders, I understand, are to go up the Hudson at night and make contact with this rebel officer, bringing him back to the sloop and so down river to Sir Henry's headquarters. There are some French troops on the rebel side and it might become necessary to interrogate French prisoners. That is why you are to be there. I think myself that, all being well, there should be no contact with the enemy at all, but it will in any event be a useful experience for you. Go on board the *Vulture* tomorrow forenoon and report for duty to Captain Sutherland, who will be expecting you."

"Am I allowed to discuss this matter with Colonel Travell, sir? I should assume that the whole story is known to him."

"Yes, he is in the secret. Not a word, however, to anyone else."

Going at once to the colonel's cabin, Delancey found him a new man, his recent depression a thing of the past.

"Action at last, Delancey! In years to come people will look back on this as the turning-point of the war. If he will accept my friend's advice, General Clinton can win the war by next year. He is a good man in many ways but he must learn to concentrate his forces and plan to achieve a decisive result in a single field. Since we have come to know each other and since I am well assured of your discretion, I shall tell you the name of this man who is about to desert the rebel cause. He is Colonel Benedict Arnold, entrusted by Washington with the defence of West Point, the principal enemy fortress on the Hudson. He is beyond question the outstanding soldier on the rebel side. Burgoyne's surrender at Saratoga was essentially brought about by Arnold. But for him the king's forces would have defeated the rebels years ago. Washington must be given the credit for keeping his army together but he has none of Arnold's brilliance as a tactician. I see the war as nearing its end."

"What I fail to understand, sir, is why a senior officer is needed for this mission."

"Because there is some kind of bargain to be struck. Arnold is sure to ask a price for changing sides. He has a weakness, you see, for money. He was deeply in debt when I knew him and lived in extravagant style among people of wealth. Yes, he will ask a price and will need to be assured of his rank in the king's army. He will expect to be brigadier-general, at least. Sir Henry's representative must have authority to conclude the terms of Arnold's appointment."

"I wonder, sir, in that event, that you were not the officer chosen."

"The matter was discussed but the view was put forward that I must not be taken prisoner. This might be regarded as a hazardous mission, alone behind the enemy lines. Apart from that, I am not on Sir Henry's staff. Arnold cannot doubt, however, that André speaks with the general's authority. He was probably the right man to choose for this rather difficult task."

When he reported next day to Captain Sutherland, Delancey was told nothing more about the operation planned for that evening. Major André came aboard that afternoon and was just as Delancey had remembered him, a good-looking and attractive young man, friendly towards junior officers—midshipmen included—and yet obviously energetic and able. Sir Henry Clinton thought very highly of him and Delancey could see why.

André went out of his way to greet all the sloop's officers and even remembered Delancey's name a year and more after the brief occasion of their only meeting. André, wearing uniform, was attended by a single servant and accompanied as far as the sloop by Colonel Beverly Robinson. They could not have been more cheerful had they been planning a picnic. Towards sunset the anchor was broken out and sail made, the sloop heading up river. As night fell careful arrangements were made to prevent any light showing on board. It was evidently the intention to pass the enemy outposts without being seen, the more possible in that the night was moonless and overcast. To navigate in these conditions was far from easy but Captain Sutherland had wisely taken a local river pilot who had known these waters since child-hood. There were lights ashore in the scattered homesteads and Delancey watched them pass and drop slowly astern as the voy-age went on. Silence had been ordered and no one spoke in more than a whisper. An hour or so before midnight there was a shortening of sail and then the sloop hove to as a boat loomed out of the darkness and came alongside. The contact had been made at the time agreed and some hours of darkness remained in which the boat could land, as arranged, at the home of Mr Joshua Hett Smith, two miles below Stoney Point. The boat moved away into the darkness but now with André on board. He might be expected to return with Arnold some time next day. There was now nothing to do but wait.

Soon after daybreak there came the sound of cannon, a sin-gle sighting shot. It was immediately followed by five other reports at irregular intervals, all echoing again from the sides of the river valley. "A six-gun battery," said *Vulture's* junior lieu-tenant. "But we know of no enemy position within miles!" No damage was done but as many cannon fired again, this time more accurately. There was a hole through the fore-topsail and a lower shroud parted on the mizen. Captain Sutherland was in a difficult position, as Delancey had to admit. He would not wish to abandon his mission, leaving André to escape as well as he could, but neither could he very well sacrifice his ship. With all this thunder of artillery the secrecy of the affair had gone. Distant bugles would be sounding the alarm, troops would be assembling and patrols would be going out in all directions. It was a question now whether André's mission was even possible. Sutherland postponed making a decision until his ship was hit for the fourth time, a cannon ball smashing the port quarter galley while another demolished the cat-head on the same side. He then raised the anchor, made sail and attempted to engage the shore battery with his port broadside. Failing to silence it, he found that the current was taking him downstream and out of range. The wind had died away and the current was taking him back to New York. In the end he went about and gained enough steerage way to gain a position well below his original anchorage at Spuyten Devil, being fired at by other rebel batteries on the way; mostly, however, at a longer range. Dropping anchor again, Captain Sutherland sent in his report. It was, essentially, a tale of disaster.

Having breakfast in the gunroom, Delancey heard different theories about what had gone wrong. "That battery was not there last month—we had no reason to expect any trouble from that headland."—"The mischief was that our anchor had dragged— we were half a mile from our intended position."—"That was not a battery position at all. We were fired upon by field guns which had parked there for the night."—"In my opinion our security was bad. The enemy had warning of what we were trying to do."

Whatever the facts, Delancey was not fated to know them. He was on board merely as a supernumerary and was presently sent back to his own ship. In the meanwhile, however, reports were coming in from the outposts and from intelligence sources. It soon became perfectly clear that Major André had been captured on his way down the river from King's Ferry, that he had been in civilian clothes by then and that he had been carrying secret documents in his boot which revealed the nature of his mission.

"My God," exclaimed Captain Sutherland, "he'll be tried as a spy, condemned and hanged!"

"What will happen then," the surgeon asked, "to the officer who was about to change sides?"

"He'll be under arrest by now," concluded the first lieutenant, "and will be hanged for treason in a matter of weeks."

Delancey returned to the *Falcon* and reported to Captain Mottram, explaining the failure in so far as he understood it. His report made, he went on to tell his story to Colonel Travell, who heard him out in silence, making the final comment "So that is that." Delancey hastened to add that the fate of Benedict Arnold was still unknown. Major André would never give him away and any captured documents would reveal only his code-name. He would most probably remain the commandant at West Point, nothing having happened to betray him.

"That is most unlikely," said Travell. "Too many people will know by now of André's mission and all the evidence leads to West Point and to a very senior officer. Sir Henry would not have sent his adjutant-general to make contact with anyone of less than colonel's rank, and who else of that rank would be at West Point? No, we must assume that Arnold's treachery—as the Americans will see it—has now been revealed. Washington may

have guessed it long ago. Others will have been able by this time
to put two and two together—his debts, his extravagances, his
marriage, his discontent over his treatment—many such circumstances point to him as to no one else. He will be under
arrest by now. With him goes my sole chance of active employment. But that is a small matter as compared with Arnold's fate.
I can say little of his character in many respects. He is vain and
petulant, greedy and self-centred, frivolous in some ways, cal-
lous in others. Place him on a battlefield, however, and he is a
genius. He goes to the root of a problem in an instant. He takes
in the whole situation while other people are still fumbling with
a spyglass and a map. He knows what move to make, what
troops to use, what leaders to appoint, what orders to issue and
at what precise time to set his forces in motion. In the field I
have seen no one like him, no one with a fraction of his leadership, ingenuity and grasp, no one who could rival him as a
commander. He could have won the war for King George and
advised ministers on how to make peace and leave us all friends
again. I see no hope of victory now nor of ending this miserable
conflict. I am sorry too for Arnold's wife, Peggy Arnold, the most
admired lady in Philadelphia—more than that, the loveliest
woman I ever saw. In real values my own Ruth is far her superior but for sheer beauty Mrs Arnold has no rival in Pennsylvania.
All Washington's young officers are in love with her, and he himself is far from blind. I could wish for her a happier future than
lies ahead of her. Somehow I cannot even imagine her being
pitied by others—she who was always the centre of attention,
the envy of all her sex. She probably never knew how much
pleasure she gave others merely by being herself."

Delancey urged Travell to restrain his grief until he actually
knew the worst but he doubted at the time whether Travell was

even listening. There was nothing to do but withdraw and leave the poor man to his misery. For the rest of the day he went about his own duties and studies but with half his mind on Travell's sense of frustration and grief. Towards evening, however, there came a welcome break in the daily routine. A boat from the dockyard came alongside with the ship's mail and there was the usual excitement over it. Some hoped to hear from their sweethearts and wives, some feared to hear from their creditors, a few expected nothing. Delancey heard from his mother at rather rare intervals and seldom from anyone else. On this occasion there was just the one letter for him and he recognised her writing at once. It was good to hear from Guernsey and to be reminded of such roots as he had. It was addressed to H.M. Ship *Falcon,* which was proof that his last letter to her had been received. He found himself wondering when he would see Guernsey again. He could be there before the end of the year if he were sent home as the admiral seemed to intend. But there was a new admiral now—Rodney himself—and his former misdeeds might be forgotten. He might be here, he supposed, for as long as the war continued. He might be at sea, in fact, for years.

Delancey's thoughts were interrupted by the sound of a shot. The officer of the watch was attempting to trace the noise, the master-at-arms was active and the marine sergeant was checking to see whether any musket had been fired. With a sense of foreboding, Delancey went at once to Colonel Travell's cabin. Knocking twice and having no answer, he entered, smelling the powder, and saw the colonel prone on the deck. There was a bullet hole through the heart and there could be no doubt that his friend was dead, the pistol lying near his hand. On the desk lay an opened letter which had presumably come with the other mail. Delancey took it up, seeing that it was dated from Philadelphia:

> Dear Colonel Travell
>
> I write to thank you for your letter but I hardly know how to answer it. You will have had good reason, no doubt, to act as you have done but you showed scant consideration for me and for your other friends. How am I to justify your actions? How am I to explain to others what I cannot myself understand?. . .

Delancey read on hastily and saw how the letter finished:

> . . . I see no object in our meeting again and I should not welcome any further letter from you. I wish you well, nevertheless, and hope that you will find pleasure in your new rank and in the company of your new friends.
>
> With regrets,
Goodbye—Ruth

Delancey replaced the letter on the desk and went to make his report.

"Mr Bancroft, sir, that shot was fired by Colonel Travell. He appears to have taken his own life."

The sequel to this tragedy came within the next few days. News came that Benedict Arnold had not been arrested following André's capture nor had he remained at West Point. He had promptly made his escape and reached the British lines. More than that, he was already in New York and in British uniform as a brigadier-general. Had Travell shown a little more patience he would have been Benedict Arnold's chief of staff with some prospect, no doubt, of further promotion. Ruth he had certainly lost but New York, as Delancey knew, was full of other girls and most of them from Tory families. Or would it be fair to conclude that Travell had always been too easily depressed, too ready to admit defeat? He had, if that were true, no great future in any case. For success in war, or in love, perhaps, a part of the secret lies in a swift recovery from disaster—so much Delancey had come to realise—and a rapid return to the battlefield. Travell had probably lacked the stamina which war demands. He had perhaps ended his misery in what was for him the only way.

If Delancey expected great things from Arnold's joining the British side he was to be disappointed. He learned from gossip that Sir Henry Clinton was extremely downcast over André's capture and predicament. He was to be hanged as a spy, that being the verdict of a court martial. There could be no doubt, however, that Washington would spare André if Clinton would return Arnold. There could be no question of that but André's fate was a bargaining point of which Washington was to make full use up to the very day of that officer's execution. This was the background to Arnold's early service on the king's side and it did nothing to strengthen his position as an adviser.

Apart from that it was soon apparent, from all Delancey could hear, that Clinton's strategy was all too fatally controlled from Whitehall. The secretary of state for the colonies was Lord George Germaine, and Clinton, like Burgoyne before him, was known to complain bitterly about the ignorant directions he received. Hearing something of this, Delancey was reminded of his earlier days in New York, when Commodore Harvey used to complain about the instructions he received from the Navy Board. He saw that the basic defect in the system was not the folly of certain individuals, foolish as they may have proved, but the mere distances between the source of authority and the scene of action. It was this distance which made the rebellion inevitable and it was this distance which made its suppression extremely difficult. Arnold knew best how to win the war but he was no match for the long-distance influence of Lord George Germaine, the man who had been cashiered for cowardice after the Battle of Minden. As from that moment Arnold was to take the field on several occasions but his career came in the end to nothing.

Delancey was now made aware that his days in the *Falcon* were numbered. A vacancy had been found for him in the sloop *Avenger* (16), which was to sail very shortly for Portsmouth.

"That ship was recently damaged," said Captain Mottram, "and is being sent home for refit, probably as escort to a small convoy. Captain Singleton has the reputation of a good seaman. It remains for me to thank you for your good service aboard the *Falcon*. You were not much of a seaman when you joined this ship and Mr Bancroft doubted whether you would ever become one. He has been proved wrong as he would be the first to admit. I have been happy to write you a letter of recommendation and I look forward to hearing of your further services. If you continue to work at your navigation as you have done during our recent voyage I should expect to see you as a lieutenant when next we meet."

"Thank you, sir. Have I leave to go ashore after being discharged from this ship?"

Captain Mottram looked doubtful, replying at last:

"My orders were positive, young man."

"Do they apply, sir, to one who is no longer a member of your ship's company?"

"I don't know that they do. I dare say, however, that Captain Singleton will have the same instructions."

"Which cannot apply, surely, until I come under his orders?"

"I see what you mean. Go ashore then—without my knowledge—wear civilian clothes while on land, keep away from the places in which you could meet your relatives and report on board the *Avenger* in three days' time. I think you have earned that much consideration. Good luck to you!"

Delancey was on shore before Captain Mottram could change his mind. Taking a room for two nights, he changed out of uniform and presently ordered the best dinner that the Jamaica Tavern could provide. He had money enough after his long penance aboard the *Falcon* and saw no reason to economise. He could have sought the company of other midshipmen but he wanted, for the moment, to escape from them. He saw in a newspaper that Charlotte de Lancey was married now to young Mr Bayard, a fact which left him strangely unmoved. He dined that day in silent luxury, thinking of all the spartan meals he had endured and would have to endure again. Next day he might hope to have female company, perhaps, but for the moment— yes, he would have cheese and dessert and a glass of port—no, two glasses of port—to crown the whole. It was luxury again to sleep in a bed and not in a hammock. But this was only a beginning—he had two more days to go and would make the most of them. Like a gentleman of independent means, he would take his ease and enjoy his leisure. What about a visit tomorrow to Brooklyn? Could he strike up an acquaintance first with some girl who was employed in a dress shop or milliner's? He was too fastidious to make any bargain with a prostitute but surely there might be a girl whose manners would pass muster but whose morals were not too strict? There was nothing hopeless about his quest and he ended with some romantic memories to dwell upon during the monastic weeks which would follow. New York was no bad town in which to spend a few days' leave. He might never see the place again but he could say, in retrospect, that he had not wasted the opportunity that was given him. Had she been blonde or brunette? Was she Susan or Sally? It is the sad fact that he could never remember.

Chapter 8

Capitulation

RICHARD landed at St Peter Port on 20 December 1780, aiming to be home for Christmas. It was bitterly cold and he made his way to the Pollet as quickly as possible.

"Richard!" his mother cried and this exclamation brought his father out from the back room.

"Welcome home!" he said in his turn, and Richard saw what effect the years had had—the spectacles, which were new, and the worried look which had grown no less.

The next hour or so were spent in mutual inquiries and assurances. Pressed by his mother, he had to admit that hardly anyone he had met in America seemed to remember Sir Edmund Andros. Then he was told, in return, of Rachel's two children, both girls, the birth of whom had made him doubly an uncle. It was now his turn to tell his father about his de Lancey relatives in America, one of them a general, no less, in the British army. While questions were asked and answered the parents and their son were taking stock of each other. Richard, at twenty, his mother could see, was a grown man, taller now and weather-beaten, with the air of one who had crossed the ocean and been under fire. He was still modest, however, and as far as ever, he explained, from achieving commissioned rank. He wore his uniform as a midshipman nevertheless and his mother could at least take pride in that. She, to him, looked much the same as ever but his father, on the second impression, looked older still, more defeated, with fewer touches of irony in his conversation which was broken by longer periods of silence. No word was said about Michael, and Richard concluded that he was himself now, for all practical purposes, their only son.

Unpacking in his attic room, Richard thought his home but little changed. The furniture was shabbier than ever, the curtains more faded, the pictures just as he had remembered them, the books a little more numerous. There was a new carpet, though, and some better china. There would have been more signs of prosperity, he reflected, if they had not placed him on the quarterdeck. That evening they sat round the fire after supper, each with a glass of brandy, and Richard told them more about the fighting in America, about New York and Rhode Island, about the situation created by the defection of Benedict Arnold. He was given in exchange the gossip of St Peter Port and news about men he could remember only as boys. One thing apparent was that King George was very much on the defensive. There was no talk now, as there had been in the early days, of what might be planned against the enemy. More fears were voiced about the enemy's possible activities during the year that was to come. Enemy ships were everywhere and even Guernsey itself seemed all too close to the coast of France.

To his mother, however, Richard's return was a significant reinforcement. "Thank God you are home safely!" she repeated. "You would know what to do if the French were sighted." Richard disclaimed omniscience but his mother went on: "And thank God you came when you did! We have a problem, Richard, and it needs an officer like you to solve it."

"I'm only a petty officer," Richard protested, "and don't expect to be anything more. But tell me what the problem is."

"Well, Richard," said his mother more slowly, "your father's business has improved of late, as you know. More forage is needed for the garrison—yes, and for the militia officers' horses as well—and we nowadays want for nothing. We are proud to think that we have a son in the navy. Your father is talked of as a possible parish officer or as a member at the least of the douzaine. So we are able these days to afford a glass of wine on occasion and sometimes, as it might be this evening, a glass of brandy or maybe a jug of rum punch which is a great comfort on a cold night. We were well supplied for Christmas, Richard, even before we knew you could be with us. Now, your father has recently bought our liquor from a friend of his, Mr Isaac Perelle, whose warehouse is in the Truchot . . ."

"And very good it is, sir," said Richard, with a slight bow towards his father, who smiled briefly and then looked sad again as he gazed into the fire.

"I should perhaps explain," his mother went on, "that Mr Perelle is not one of the regular wine merchants. He is what we call a free-trader, no different in truth from the others but trading in rather a small way, through friends in Jersey. No harm in it, of course, but not a business to discuss too openly—not at least in time of war. I am sure you take my meaning."

"I quite understand, mother," said Richard with a smile. "You are forgetting that I was brought up here!"

"So you were, to be sure, and had your eyes open all the while. Well, then. Isaac Perelle has friends in St Malo who sometimes come over here on business. He has one of them staying with him at this very moment, a Monsieur Layard, a genteel man with a very good name in the trade. Your father met him the other evening and was told that Jersey may be attacked by the French at any time!"

"Perhaps, ma'am," said the patient Mr Delancey, "you would

do better to let me tell my own story, with more hope maybe of telling it correctly."

"Oh, well, Mr Delancey, if you are to mount your high horse . . . ! I am sure that I have told Richard all that is of any consequence."

"No doubt, ma'am. Allow me to explain, Richard, that Monsieur Layard had been very hospitably entertained that evening and talked with a freedom that amazed me. I had gone there merely to discuss a small matter of business but Mr Perelle made me come in and meet his guest. They were neither of them sober and Monsieur Layard was hardly able to stand. While in this state he spoke at length, though not always distinctly, of a body of troops now collected, by his account, near Granville. He thought poorly of the men, who were volunteers from different regiments; bad characters, in other words, discarded by their officers or seeking to escape the consequences of their ill-behaviour. He claimed to have talked with the leader of the force, the Baron de Rullecour, who had previously served under the Prince of Nassau; a good officer, he said, but ruined by gambling and desperate to recover his fortunes. The baron talked openly of his plan for capturing Jersey and boasted that he was to be the governor."

"But all this talk seems excessively imprudent," said Richard. "Why should this Frenchman warn you in advance of what his king intended?"

"Why, indeed? The impression I gained was that Perelle had spoken, half in jest, of the mock-hostility that exists between this island and Jersey. Taking him too seriously, Monsieur Layard had come to suppose that the capture of Jersey would be actually welcome here as giving Guernsey the whole of a trade in which we now have to share."

"Did he give you any idea of the numbers?"

"He spoke of thousands but only very generally and vaguely."

"So what did you decide to do, sir?"

"After warning Mr Perelle, I reported what I knew to the bailiff. He dismissed it at once, saying that he heard such a rumour every week."

"But you still think, sir, that the report should be taken seriously?"

"Well, Richard, I think the governor of Jersey should be warned. This French expedition has also been spoken of in the market-place. There is more than a chance that something is intended."

"Everyone knows about it!" Mrs Delancey exclaimed with animation. "There are thousands of men at St Malo and we may be murdered in our beds for all the bailiff cares! I really have no patience with that sort of man. The king should be told and the militia should stand to arms. If James Andros were still alive the South Regiment would be paraded now!"

"No doubt of it," said Richard. "Are there no men-of-war here or in Jersey?"

"Of course not!" said Richard's mother. "Everyone knows that we have hardly ships enough to defend our coasts. We see none here for weeks at a time and Jersey, I'll swear, is as ill-protected. I can't think what the king's ministers have been doing all these years—nothing, certainly, to save us from invasion."

"We see little of the king's ships," Mr Delancey agreed, "but I hear that a sloop is expected here presently, with despatches, I believe, for the governor. We could hardly expect her to fight the French single-handed."

"She would at least bring a sea officer to whom I could report. I doubt whether an army officer would listen to either of us."

His parents had to agree with Richard that their best plan would be to wait for the sloop's arrival.

"But she won't sail before Christmas," said Richard. "She'll spend the next few days in harbour, that's certain. I never heard of a man-of-war putting to sea on Christmas Eve."

The elder Delanceys could see the logic of that and hoped that the same reasoning would apply to the French.

At the Town Church on Christmas Day Richard could sense some change in attitude towards his father, several merchants greeting him and one, who shook hands, was (his mother explained in a whisper) a constable, no less, of the parish. During the sermon Richard thought again of the threatened invasion. Should he try to meet Layard? But then, he had himself been seen in uniform, and Perelle would have warned Layard against talking too much. There was nothing to do but wait. They had a goose that day for dinner and a bottle of claret and they rewarded with warm ale the carol-singers who came to the door. Later that evening they had rum punch and Richard gave his parents a few small gifts he had brought from America. Then they talked again about the war and the colonies.

Mrs Delancey had no patience with the colonists, who seemed to have no sense of gratitude. "If only Sir Edmund were still alive," she sighed, "the war would soon be brought to an end."

From what he had heard, Richard thought that Sir Edmund's presence would have made matters infinitely worse. He kept that idea to himself, however, and spoke again of the de Lanceys of New York. But his mother would not allow that the other side of the family could be of interest.

"I have never understood," she declared, "why people should go to settle in America. To live there for a time—say as governor of Virginia—is well enough but to make one's home there is not at all the fashion. Now if only Prince Rupert had been alive, in the place of that General Sage or Rage, the war would have been ended by now and that odious Mr Washington would be a prisoner in the Tower of London. I can't conceive what our generals have been thinking of."

The sloop *Ariel* (18 guns) came into the roads on 2 January and saluted the castle. She was commanded, it seemed, by Captain Fearnside, who was in a hurry to return to Portsmouth. Richard was rowed out to her and reported to the officer of the watch. He was presently standing to attention before the captain, an intense young man who listened to his story in silence. When Richard had finished, Fearnside took out a chart from the drawer of his desk and began to study it. Still without saying a word he made some calculations on a piece of paper. He finally laid back and stared fixedly at Richard. After what seemed an age he finally spoke, first telling Richard to stand at ease.

"This report is almost certainly untrue and I will tell you why. First, this is the wrong time of year for the attempt described. Second, a force of at least six thousand men—and more probably eight thousand—would be needed for an attack on Jersey. No such expedition—troops, ships, artillery, supplies—could be assembled without our coming to know about it from a dozen different sources; and we have no such intelligence. Third, the story is of the sort that enemy agents put about, drawing our attention away from the place that is actually threatened. But for one word I should dismiss your report as rubbish. I would not say that you were wrong to make it but the report—save for one word—sounds totally false." Captain Fearnside paused for another long minute, staring at Richard as before. "The word which rings true is Rullecour. There *is* such an officer, I believe, and he *is* a gambler. No one but a gambler would make the attempt you describe." After another pause the captain asked one other question: "Where will they land?"

"I have no idea, sir."

"But you *should* have an idea. Put yourself in the enemy's place. You embark at Granville after dark. Where will you land?" He pushed the chart over to Richard, who looked at it for a minute and then replied:

"In Grouville Bay."

"Just so. And then?"

"March on St Helier and attack the town at daybreak."

"Or is that too risky?"

"I am a gambler, sir."

"So you are. All at stake on a single throw. You have told me *where*. Now tell me *when*."

"Not with this wind, sir."

"Nor'-west? . . . No."

"When the wind comes north-easterly, sir, with a falling tide in the hour before dawn."

"Right. Now listen to me, young man. I don't believe this report but I shall act almost as if I did. When the wind serves I shall sail for Granville and sweep round the bay. Finding nothing, as I fully expect, I shall put you ashore at Gorey. You can then report to the lieutenant-governor while I head back for Portsmouth. I shall send for you before I sail. Tell the officer of the watch where you are to be found."

"Aye, aye, sir."

That was the end of the interview and Richard was soon ashore again, feeling suddenly several years older. He had learnt more about war in ten minutes than he had learnt in as many months aboard the *Romney*. Fearnside was clever, there could be no doubt of that, but he had seemed feverish, as if aware that

his life would be short. Did people really have such a premoni-
tion? He was still pondering this question when he reached
home. He told his parents that he was being sent to warn the
authorities at Jersey, would go in the *Ariel* and return by the
ordinary packet. He and his parents would at least have done
their best.

The wind veered easterly on the evening of 4 January and
the *Ariel* sailed with Richard aboard, scouring the French coast
from Carteret down to Cancale. There appeared to be no unusual
activity at Granville or St Malo and Fearnside headed north again
on the evening of the 5th. He was off Gorey nearly an hour after
midnight and gave Richard a letter addressed to the lieutenant-
governor. "That will admit you to the presence," he said, "and
it is as much as I can do to help you. The boat's alongside and
I wish you good luck."

After Richard had been landed in Gorey harbour, replying to
the challenge of a sleepy sentinel, the *Ariel* sailed on northwards
with the wind abeam, passing Alderney on her passage for home.
Richard, meanwhile, turned his back on the looming towers of
Mont Orgueil Castle and set off to reach St Helier. There were
two ways of doing that—as he knew—one over the higher
ground through Five Oaks and St Saviours, the other on lower
ground through Grouville and La Grange, and both implying a
five-mile walk. It was a cold and moonless night with the
wind still easterly, the surf heavy along the shore and the neap
tide high but falling. He chose the lower road, walking briskly
to keep warm, and reflected that the conditions would have
been right for a landing in Grouville Bay. All was quiet there,
however, and he pressed on, huddled in his cloak and glad to
have the wind at his back. The Grouville church clock struck
two as he approached and he was challenged a minute later by

a sentry who presently called out the guard from an adjacent barn. The sergeant, suspicious and surly, sent Richard under escort to a house called La Fontaine where, he said, the officers were to be found. So they were and awake, not from any excess of zeal but because they had been playing cards. The senior officer present was Lieutenant James Robertson. There was a bottle on the table, probably not the first, and the game had just finished when Richard was brought to the door. After listening to Richard's account of himself, Robertson sent the two soldiers back to their post and asked Richard to join him at the table.

"A glass of wine, Mr Delancey? So ye seek to warn us that the French are on their way?"

"Yes, sir. I think that the lieutenant-governor should be told at once. I believe that I could reach Elizabeth Castle within the hour."

"Sit down, man, and be easy. Ye'll no' be finding the governor at the Castle. He bides in La Motte House, St James's Street. But ye'll get no thanks, I'm thinking, if ye rouse him at this hour."

"Shouldn't he be told at once, sir?"

"What have ye to tell him, man? That there are French at Granville? That this is the sort of nicht they might have a mind to come over? Let it bide 'till the morning."

Seeing the force of this, Richard accepted wine and took a chair. Robertson soon afterwards sent the two ensigns off to bed.

"The bairns will be wanting their sleep, Mr Delancey . . . Your news will wait for ye've nought to tell us and yon Major Corbet will no' be sounding the alarm as yet. I doubt he'd do anything if the French were here."

"I should expect a lieutenant-governor to be more than a major. What sort of man is he?"

"Corbet? A fine tall figure of a man. Ye'll no' see one better on parade. A braw commander is yon Corbet—and empty as a drum. And he being major, none else can be mair. Our garrison is all detachments—two or three companies under a captain, a half battalion under a junior major. Here we've part of the 83rd under gude auld Captain Campbell—the regiment was raised in Glasgow. We do nothing but mount guard. We don't even watch the Plat Rocque Point, with the four guns mounted there. I fretted at first, ye ken, but now I leave things be."

Robertson pronounced the name of his immediate senior as "Cawmell" and Richard sensed a hint of scorn. He learnt more about the garrison over the next hour or so. There were artillerymen and engineers at Elizabeth Castle under Captain Aylward; the 78th (Highland) Regiment, or some of it, under Captain Lumsden, stationed in the western outskirts of St Helier; and some of the 95th Regiment further out in St Peter's Parish. There were three thousand or more, with thousands of militia as well, but no sort of plan for defending the place.

"It's as well, sir, that the French don't know the state of the island," said Richard finally but the soured lieutenant would not agree.

"Why shouldna they ken? There's trade with St Malo with comings and goings, and yon Corbet taking his share. Where d'ye think this wine comes frae?"

Richard finally spent the rest of the night at La Fontaine, sleeping on the floor until roused by Robertson, who had been visiting his sentinels.

"Is all well, sir?" asked Richard.

"I dinna ken," said Robertson, warming his hands at what remained of the fire. "There's dogs barking to the westward. There's something astir that way." He called for his servant to make tea and call the other officers. "It's near seven," he said.

"We'll stand to in half an hour." He had hardly spoken before there came the sound of a galloping horse. Robertson was outside in an instant, with Richard at his heels. It was still pitch dark but Richard could see that the sentinels were alert with muskets at the ready.

Nearer came the sound and then, quite suddenly, the horseman was reining up in front of them.

"Who goes there?" demanded the sentinel.

"Captain Hemery of the Town Militia."

"What's the password?"

"Elizabeth."

"Pass, friend. All's well."

"All's well be damned—where's Captain Campbell?"

At this point Robertson spoke up. "At Fort Conway, sir. I'm Robertson of the 83rd. Wad you tell me what's happened?"

"I'll tell you, by God. The French have landed and have captured St Helier!"

The militia officer galloped on to Fort Conway and Robertson turned to Richard. "Your warning came too late, laddie!" A minute later he was shouting for the colour-sergeant and telling the sentinel to fire in the air. "Aye, that'll rouse them!" he muttered. "On parade, colour-sergeant, and give out ball cartridge. Drummer—sound the alarm!"

Grouville came alive with lights in the windows and doors opening, men cursing and dogs barking. Then the drum rolled and the half-company began to fall in. Sergeants called the roll and ensigns inspected the muskets. Ten minutes later and soon after the half-company had been reported present and correct, came the sound of the guns. Cannon were firing at St Helier, that much was obvious. Richard wondered what he should do next. His original errand had become pointless and it remained for him to make himself useful—but where and how? He was still wondering when the sound came of another galloping horse. This time it was a civilian and one merely anxious to escape from the French. Robertson questioned him about the numbers of the enemy but he vaguely replied, "Thousands!" To the further question, however, "Where did they land?" his answer was more explicit: "At La Rocque Point, seemingly. They marched in through the Colomberie."

After this informant had gone, Robertson turned to Richard in despair. "My God—d'ye see what this means? They landed under our verra noses! The 83rd let them through! We're disgraced for ever." Richard could see very well what he meant. But he remembered the chart and thought to himself that a landing at La Rocque Point was lunacy. "I must report to the captain," said Robertson. "And you had best come with me, Mr Delancey. Mr Fraser, I leave you in command." By the time they had found Captain Campbell and made their respective reports, it was just beginning to get light. The sound of the guns had died away and all was oddly quiet.

Captain Campbell turned out to be very much as Richard had pictured him—elderly, pot-bellied and indecisive. "I can't quit my post here," he said several times. "Not without orders." His sergeant-major said something about marching towards the sound of the guns. "When ordered, yes. But I don't know what the situation is." Then Robertson intervened: "You would likely know more, sir, if you sent a wee patrol down to La Rocque Point."

"But then orders might come and I not able to march until the patrol returned."

The discussion continued but always returned to the same

point: Captain Campbell would do nothing without an order from someone senior to him. The group had been reduced to an irritated silence when their deliberations were interrupted by an extraordinary apparition. Out of the morning mist came two nine-pounder cannon pushed laboriously by a motley group of rustics and followed by a horse-drawn box-cart. In command was a bellicose and excited clergyman, who presently introduced himself as the Rev. Le Couteur, Rector of St Martin's. The cannon were his own property, he said, the artillerymen his own parishioners. They had pushed the cannon over two miles (largely downhill) and wanted only to be shown the enemy! Why a clergyman should possess artillery was, and remained, a mystery, but Campbell had only a tepid welcome for this timely reinforcement. He told the rector to rest his men and supply them, if he could, with breakfast. The word having given him an idea, he then dismissed his own men to breakfast but with orders to parade again in an hour's time. By then, he prayed inwardly, someone would have told him what to do. The only suggestion he accepted was one made by Robertson, that the other half-company should be brought from Grouville, bringing the whole detachment together. This was done, the total strength amounting, Richard guessed, to perhaps two hundred.

It was light by now and refugees began to come in from St Helier, a few with horses and carts but mostly on foot, straggling in parties of five or six. They had much to say for themselves and some had actually seen the French. A young English-speaking tailor, who lived in Queen Street, had seen Major Corbet taken prisoner. Others taken with him were Mr Durell, Mr Hogg and Mr Chariton. They had all been taken by surprise. They were being held in the Court House.

"Would there be any firing when ye left?" asked Robertson.

"No, sir. There was firing at first, which woke us all, and that was the town guard being overcome. There was none after that."

"But we heard cannon . . .?"

"That was from the castle, sir, and fired, I reckon, to give the alarm."

"How many Frenchmen would there be?"

"I couldn't rightly say. We left, you see, in the dark. But I was told by a neighbour that five thousand had landed and that another ten thousand are on their way from St Malo."

"Were the French pillaging the town?"

"No, sir, not that I saw."

"But you fled for safety?"

"My wife's expecting, sir."

"Where are you going then?"

"To my cousin's at Gorey."

Other refugees were less coherent, talking vaguely about atrocities they had not witnessed but of which they had been told. Robertson, using Richard as interpreter when necessary, heard much the same story from others with the addition of some tale about Elizabeth Castle which might, by one account, be still in British hands. Several other folk repeated the story of the ten thousand Frenchmen on their way from St Malo. With St Helier in French hands they would at least have a harbour at which to land.

"Weel," said Robertson finally, "there is nae much doot that St Helier has fallen, but as to the enemy's strength I canna mak sense o' it."

"Nor I," said Richard, "but this talk of an army on the way is rubbish."

"And for why, Mr Delancey?"

"They could've assembled such a force without our hearing of it." (Richard remembered of Captain Fearnside's words.)

"Maybe they couldna at that. But what have they ashore already?"

"If I saw their flotilla, sir, I could make a guess."

"Is it that easy, man?"

"I have served in conjunct expeditions, sir."

Richard realised, in saying this, that he was talking too much like a navy captain. He added quickly, "Only a rough guess."

Robertson smiled suddenly: "I'm thinking, laddie, that you'll some day mak a gude officer."

Things remained at a standstill for another hour or so. The church clock struck nine and Richard had the sickening sense of time being wasted. He had often been told, and now firmly believed, that to do nothing in war is nearly always wrong. Campbell made his men fall in again and carried out another inspection of their muskets. It was still bitterly cold with the wind in the east and more than a hint of rain. Campbell's horse was being led up and down by his orderly. When stood at ease, the soldiers stamped to warm their feet. The only other noise was the distant cry of the gulls.

At about half past nine came the sound of a horse at the trot. Then a mounted officer came in sight, was challenged and allowed to pass, and finally reined up in front of Campbell.

"Lieutenant Snow, sir, of the militia." He saluted stiffly. "I have a letter for you, sir, from the lieutenant-governor." He pulled the letter from his greatcoat pocket and handed it over.

Campbell tore it open and read it aloud for the benefit of his officers:

To the commanding officer of the 83rd Regiment.

St Helier, 6 Jan. 1781

The island being surprised, to save the town from being destroyed and obtain certain privileges to the inhabitants, the lieutenant-governor hath signed the capitulation; the troops are to march with the honours of war, the militia are to be quiet and hostilities are to cease.

M. Corbet, Lt.-Gov.

Enclosed with this letter was another page in the same handwriting but with no signature.

The regular and militia are not to fire till further orders.

Looking round at the others, Campbell said solemnly: "So that is that, gentlemen. Major Corbet has capitulated and we must obey orders. Tell the parade to dismiss, Mr Robertson, but no man to leave barracks."

As this order was obeyed the militia officer saluted and rode off towards Gorey, carrying similar letters, no doubt, for other military posts between Mont Orgueil and Rozel.

Campbell led his officers indoors with the intention of explaining to them the difference between "capitulation" and "surrender." He knew, none better, the etiquette of warfare. Richard followed the others in, uninvited but no one questioning his right to be there. They were all, at that moment, too stunned to question anything. Captain Campbell stood with his back to the fire, looking happier than he had done since daybreak. He was no coward but he liked to be told what he had to do. Here were his orders—and, better still, *written* orders—which he could produce at any subsequent court martial. How right he had been to stay where he was! Any action he could have taken would have been in flat contradiction of the order he had since received; an order indeed which he had rather cleverly anticipated.

"You will be as grieved as I am, gentlemen, that the campaign should have ended like this. Our duty, however, is clear, and you must all obey orders to the letter. First—"

It was going to be a good lecture but it stopped at that point. Captain Campbell knew his duty (none better) but there was one factor—or, rather, one person—he had overlooked. He had forgotten about the rector of St Martin's.

Chapter 9

BATTLE OF ST HELIER

THE ENTRANCE of the Rev. Francis Le Couteur had all the impact of an exploding bomb. At one moment Captain Campbell was about to make a speech. An instant later he was fighting for his life. The rector of St Martin's was not a big man but he seemed at that moment to fill the room, everyone else being pushed against the walls by the mere force of his personality. "*What* is this?" he shouted as he stormed in. "Do I hear aright—that you have *surrendered?* That you have laid down your arms without firing a shot?" Reeling under this frontal attack, Campbell said that he had the lieutenant-governor's order to cease fire.

"Major Corbet's order? But he is no longer governor! He is no longer *anything!* He is on his knees to the French now and will be on his knees before a court martial afterwards. Mr Corbet is finished for ever. Let's hear no more rubbish about orders from *him!*"

"But I have his orders in writing, sir—orders from my superior officer."

"Let me see them!"

"Very well, sir. Read them for yourself."

The clergyman looked them over and returned to the charge. "He signed that meaningless nonsense with a French sword at his throat. And the other sheet he hasn't signed at all."

"I have my orders, sir."

"Fiddlesticks! You wear a sword, don't you? Then use it, man! Drive this pack of rascals out of the island!"

"My force is too weak for that."

"It's *you* who are too weak! You'll leave all the fighting to the 95th, will you?"

"But they have the *same* orders!"

"And do you think Major Peirson is the man to obey them? You have met him, surely? You have spoken with him, haven't you? Can you see him agreeing to *surrender?*"

"But the governor—"

"Stop bleating about the governor. We have none. All we have is a pack of cowardly French waiting for you to destroy them."

"But—but—"

"But nothing. March on St Helier! Don't waste another instant. Every moment is precious! Into battle, man, or you'll go down in history as a coward."

That Campbell should have resisted this onslaught is incredible but he did so, shaking his head and seeking refuge in his bedroom. The rector turned at once to Mr Robertson.

"Now's *your* opportunity! Take command and march into St Helier. You have the chance to be famous!"

"I have the chance to be cashiered, sir. I micht no' heed the governor's order but I canna supersede the captain. That would finish me in the regiment."

"Look, Mr Robertson. I'm a man of some property. If you lose your commission, I'll make it up to you."

"It's mair than that, sir. Na, I canna do as you ask. I'm under orders, ye see."

"But I am *not!*" said Richard, speaking for the first time since entering the room.

"You are junior to me, Mr Delancey."

"I am not, sir."

"You'll do as you're told!"

"I'll do as I please. Reverend sir, I'm with you. Shall we go?"

They left together and the clergyman looked at him in wonder: "What about your career?"

"I have been a midshipman, sir, but I have no ship at present and am merely a private individual with some knowledge of cannon. I suggest we take your guns into battle."

"And so we shall! We'll reach St Helier in an hour."

"No, sir. By your leave, I can offer you a better target close at hand. The vessels off La Rocque Point in which the French came! Leave St Helier to the 95th and cut off the French retreat."

"You're a man after my own heart. Let's have those guns on their way!"

Ten minutes later the small column started off, headed by the rector. His parishioners present numbered twenty-two, enough to keep the guns moving and drive the cart which carried the ammunition. But Richard was concerned to find that they were all unarmed. He also realised that the men were far from their own parish and unfamiliar, therefore, with the ground. He was relieved, therefore, when he saw three militiamen coming towards him, muskets in hand.

"Where are you going?" he asked in French.

They explained that they were going to Grouville to join up with their company of the East Regiment.

"Have you seen the French?" asked the rector.

"Yes, sir—with guns and all, with boats and ships."

"Then lead us towards them."

"But, sir—our company—"

"Your company will be coming this way—so you can save yourself the walk."

With some difficulty the militiamen were persuaded to march towards the enemy. After an hour's march Richard stopped the column, explaining to his clergyman friend that the time had come to do some scouting.

"We must find the right position from which to open fire."

"But if we stop here, we shall be wasting time."

"No, sir. We'll waste more time if we take the wrong path. And we'll ruin all if the French see us coming."

There was no time to explain at length but the Rev. M. Le Couteur luckily took his word for it and his men were more than glad of the rest.

"Come with me," said Richard to the militiamen.

As they marched on, Richard tried to explain what he wanted; a position from which two guns could be brought into action. It had to be approached unseen, with a hollow behind it for the ammunition cart. It had to offer a clear field of fire and a good view of the target. He doubted at the end whether they had the least idea of what he was talking about. They muttered among themselves, however, and one of them presently offered to act as guide. Following a path to the left under his guidance and passing through a gap in the wall on their right, they presently came out in a field near a farmhouse. Below them and less than a mile distant was the Plat Rocque Battery, in enemy hands. To the left and further away was the flotilla, at anchor, from which the French had landed. The exposed position where he was would not serve, although admittedly within range, but there was another and slightly higher hillock further forward and on his right, surmounted by a wall made of loose granite. After a few minutes of hurried inspection he decided that this was the place. He marked the gun positions, on flat ground, twenty yards apart and left a militiaman at each with orders to make a gap in the wall about four feet wide. With the third militiaman (the guide) he hurried back to the point where the Rev. M. Le Couteur was waiting impatiently. The order was given to advance and another half-hour saw the cannon manhandled into position behind the wall, each with its own embrasure.

The panting rustics sat down to recover their breath. The bellicose gentleman produced a spyglass from his pocket and glared through it at the captured battery position. The French had shifted the guns so as to fire inland and were at work on a breast-work to flank them.

"There are not more than a hundred of them!" he exclaimed. "Let's open fire at once!"

Richard asked to borrow the spyglass and kept it to his eye for several minutes, much to his fuming companion's annoyance.

"That I should have lived to see the French ashore in St Clement's parish, walking back and forth as if the island belonged to them!"

Richard handed back the spyglass and began to scratch on some bare earth with a twig.

"There are 24 vessels at anchor and eleven boats drawn up on the beach. Some other boats were evidently wrecked in landing, probably with some loss of life. All the craft in sight are quite small, of a hundred tons or less. Allowing for ammunition and supplies, they will each have carried forty men in addition to the crew. That comes to nine hundred and sixty but we'll call it a thousand. Less a hundred here, that gives us nine hundred Frenchmen in St Helier. I suspect, however, that they lost a hundred, say, in landing, which puts their army at eight hundred. That is the approximate size of the force we have to destroy."

"Then let's about it!" cried the rector, fairly dancing with impatience.

"Yes, sir. But will you be so good as to go back to Captain Campbell and tell him what the position is? There are only eight hundred of the enemy in St Helier and a hundred here. I submit that he destroy these first and then march to town."

"Do you mean to propose, sir, that I absent myself from the action—I whose cannon you have just trained on the enemy? I, but for whom you would have no guns at all? Is that, sir, your serious proposition?"

"No, sir. We shan't fire until you return."

"What—losing another hour?"

"You have to realise, sir, that I have to teach your men how to fire cannon. If they are taught nothing they will blow themselves up. I need half an hour with them before we fire a shot."

"Very well, young man. But don't dare to begin without me! On second thoughts, you will lack the means. I have the flint and steel in my pocket"

"Very well, sir. Take this militiaman with you as orderly. And bring back any others you may happen to meet. With only two, I think myself short of infantry!"

Richard plunged into gunnery instruction as the rector strode off. To train a real gun-crew took months of work, as he knew, but that meant rapidity of fire. It would be enough for his present purpose if he could teach them to fire without hurting themselves. Looking at them critically, he realised for the first time that they were all either old or young. Those of military age would all be in the militia. As against that, the old men must all have *been* in the militia. "Which of you has fired a cannon before?" he asked, and, to his relief, three of the men stepped forward. One had been in the militia artillery and the other two had been at sea. He formed two gun-crews, each with a captain, numbered them off and told them the sequence.

"First the cartridge—ram it *right* home seam-downwards—then the wad—then the shot, rammed *well in*—now the other wad—the ramrod again. Now we have the gun loaded. The gun-captain pricks the cartridge—like this—through the touch-hole. Then he fills the touch-hole with priming powder, so. The gun is now primed and ready to fire. But we've forgotten something. What is it, somebody?"

"You haven't lit the slow match, sir," said the ex-militia artilleryman.

"Nor I have; and I won't for the present. What else?"

"We need water, sir."

"Right! You two young men—double off to the farm down there and come back with two buckets of water. Quick! Off with you!" The two boys scampered off and Richard went on with the lesson.

"The gun-captain applies the linstock—like this, but with the match lit. When he does this you all step back out of the way and so does he. The gun fires! Now we push the worm—this thing—down the barrel, to clean it. Then the sponge, for which we need the water. After that we can reload, starting all over again." He paused and asked, "Is that clear?" The men nodded and muttered "Yes" or "Clear enough," so he went on: "Very well then, we know what to do. We have now to know which task will be for whom." He numbered them off, allocated the duties and began the first exercise. By the fourth repetition it was correctly, if slowly, performed. After the sixth, the two boys returned with buckets of water and were then given the task of fetching the ammunition from the cart, thirty yards in rear.

"Can't we have the cart nearer, sir?" asked one of them. "We shouldn't have so far to go."

"No you wouldn't," said Richard. "But if the enemy fire back and hit that cart, I don't want to be sitting on it—do you?" There was a laugh at this and Richard decided to give his men a rest. They were still resting when the Rev. M. Le Couteur reappeared. With him came Lieutenant Helier Godfray and seven of his men from the East Regiment. With him also came the best of news:

"Mr Robertson is on his way to join us with half of the 83rd!"

"What—did you persuade Captain Campbell?"

"No, sir, I did not. But I said this to him: 'If Mr Robertson marched off without orders from you, would you look the other way, knowing nothing about it?' He agreed to that and the troops are ten minutes or so behind us. Now for my cannon!"

For the rector of St Martin's the great moment of the day had come. He personally lit the slow match and then looked over the wall, peering through his spyglass to see what progress the French had made with their breastwork. There was little more accomplished, as he pointed out.

"You see, sir," said Richard, "that battery was made to face the other way. To turn it round is no easy task."

"And they have no more time in which to do it."

"Will you watch, sir, and tell us where the shot falls?"

To this plan the rector readily agreed and Richard, after finally checking the aim, called out the order: "Number One Gun—Fire!"

There was a loud bang and the rector, watching, shouted back the result:

"Too far! It fell in the sea and somewhat to the left."

"Number Two Gun—Fire!"

The bang was quickly followed by another correction.

"Too far! In the sea and still further to the left."

It was to be expected that the French, with four cannon, would reply. They had men enough round the guns but they seemed to achieve nothing. Not being themselves under fire, Richard's gun-crews went on stolidly, altering elevation and bearing until Number One Gun's fourth round destroyed one of the French boats. Number Two Gun then hit another, Number One Gun a third. The boats drawn up on the beach were slowly being reduced to matchwood but not a Frenchman had been hit.

"What's this?" shouted the clergyman with the spyglass. "Why don't you destroy the enemy?"

"It's better, sir," said Richard, "to deprive them of their means of escape."

After hearing some more ecclesiastical grumbling, Richard resumed his methodical bombardment. Then he yelled, *"Cease fire!"* and told the gun-captain of Number Two Gun that his ramrod had not gone home. "For God's sake don't fire with the ball half-way up the barrel. You'll burst the gun and kill yourselves. Do it slowly and do it *right!"* Then he saw that Number One Gun had several cartridges lined up and ready to use. He had them taken back to the cart. "Don't have more than one cartridge at a time." The fire was slow and inaccurate, Richard being chiefly intent on the safety precautions. Apart from that, his own knowledge was minimal—as he knew—and he had never commanded a battery before. In one respect, however, he was achieving results. Several of the vessels previously at anchor were making sail, evidently to withdraw out of range. The escape of the French troops ashore was gradually becoming impossible and their reinforcement highly unlikely. The Frenchmen round La Rocque Point were in a trap. It remained for the 83rd to go in with the bayonet.

As Richard joined the rector for a moment, borrowing his spyglass, he suddenly found Lieutenant Robertson beside him.

"Weel done, Reverend, sir!" said the Scotsman, snatching the spyglass. "We've just heard that Peirson of the 95th is marching on St Helier! The captain is on my heels with the ither half of the 83rd, having taken time to send Peirson news of what he means to do. I'll go to the right and take them in flank."

Up came Lieutenant Godfray who asked, "May we come with you?"

This offer was accepted at once and Robertson went back to meet his men, with ten militiamen to add to his detachment. Richard now shifted his aim, firing directly on the French position and on the flank which Robertson meant to turn. The aim was as poor as ever but the French began to sustain casualties, much to the rector's satisfaction.

"Well aimed, Mr Delancey! We'll teach these fellows a lesson!"

"Yes, sir. Here beginneth the Second Lesson!"

"Shame on you, sir. Don't mock the Book of Common Prayer."

"Wouldn't dream of it, sir. Number One Gun—*Fire!*"

"Short and to the right," said the rector. "Whom the Lord loveth he chasteneth . . ."

Over to the right Richard could now see Robertson's column advancing to the attack. He had formed his men into two platoons and was leading the first himself, sword in hand. Richard ceased fire as the infantry went in, then opened a long-range and ineffective bombardment of the flotilla. Watching from the wall, he and the rector saw Robertson's column halt, fire a volley and then assault with the bayonet. As he did so Captain Campbell arrived with his column, passed just to the left of Richard's position, and made a frontal attack on the French breastwork. He came too late, however. Robertson had routed the French before Campbell's attack could develop; not without casualties, though, on his side, Lieutenant Godfray being among the wounded. After

a half-hearted attempt to re-embark, the enemy mostly surrendered. Under a distant fire from Richard's cannon what remained
of the French flotilla hoisted sail and made off eastwards, leaving the Baron de Rullecour to his fate.

"Half-past twelve," said the rector. "The battle is over. And
that has been the finest sight I shall ever see. I think, sometimes,
that I chose the wrong vocation."

Congratulating the clergyman and thanking his parishioners,
Richard suggested to them that they should march for home.
This they did, after giving three cheers, and Richard went forward to view the battlefield. There he found Campbell very
much in command and not on the best of terms with Robertson. And now, to crown all, he had received a letter from Major
Peirson, ordering him to bring the 83rd to Gallows Hill on the
far side of St Helier.

"It's impossible," Campbell said. "My men are exhausted and
I have seventy prisoners to guard." Seeing that the French had
provided themselves with horses, now going spare, Richard
offered to ride with any message that the captain wished to
send. Campbell accepted the offer with gratitude. "I'd have sent
Robertson but you can see that he is shifting the guns back into
position. I suppose that he's right but I wish he'd wait for orders.
Anyway, my compliments to Major Peirson. I have received his
orders and will obey them as soon as possible. You can tell him
yourself what the position is and that we have fifteen men killed
or wounded."

Richard was an indifferent horseman at best. Choosing what
he hoped was the quietest animal and arming himself with a cutlass taken from one of the enemy dead, he set off at a trot and
reached the St Clement's Road via the Rue de Chausey. He was
about three miles, he learnt, from St Helier but that was not his

destination. To reach Gallows Hill, with St Helier in enemy hands, he would have to circle the town to the northwards. He had no idea how to do that but neither was he very confident about his errand. Peirson must have sent that message hours ago and the situation would have changed since then. The chances were that the 95th would be somewhere else by now. His doom was seemingly to go on one fool's errand after another and this one was the more foolish in that Campbell had not the slightest intention of obeying the order, being careful to avoid a written reply, probably with the intention of denying afterwards that he had received the order in the first place. Or was that unfair? He would clearly not march in the immediate future—"as soon as possible" was the phrase he had used, reassuring but vague. There was a sense, indeed, in which Campbell was right. At La Rocque Point he was well placed to cut off the French retreat—supposing that their flotilla were to return—while it would take him hours to reach Gallows Hill, supposing that he could get there at all.

As Richard approached St Helier he was made uneasy by the prevailing silence. The inhabitants were in their cellars or had fled. There was no sound of firing, no sound at all save for the echo of his horse's hooves from the cottage walls. He turned off to the right, thinking that he would have to circle the town that way but half expecting to come across a French barricade. There was no sign of the French, however, and he turned left again into what he found afterwards was the Colomberie. There he dismounted, moving forwards cautiously as a church clock struck one. Then, quite suddenly, a group of British infantry crossed the road at the double from right to left. These were followed by another group marching rapidly and led by an officer on foot. From somewhere ahead in the town came the sudden boom of a cannon, the noise of which proved too much for Richard's mount. The reins were jerked from Richard's hands as the horse plunged and reared. A moment later it had gone with a clatter, heading back the way it had come and probably towards its stable. Richard walked on and came to the point at which the redcoats had crossed the Colomberie. Just round the corner on his right he came across a young ensign waiting impatiently for his men to catch up with him. Richard introduced himself as a messenger from the 83rd and asked where Major Peirson was to be found.

"The French are round the Royal Court and Major Peirson is going to attack them from the other side—from Gallows Hill and past the hospital. He has sent us, the light company of the 78th, to occupy the Mont de la Ville and cut off the enemy's retreat. The light company of the 95th is behind us and some militia as well. Hurry up, there! Sergeant, tell those men to keep on the move!"

Richard concluded that the delivery of his message would be a waste of time. The French were surrounded already and the presence or absence of the 83rd would make no difference at all. Nor would Peirson be gratified at this moment for information about the skirmish at La Rocque Point. He had his opponents in a trap and was closing in for the kill. There could be only eight hundred Frenchmen at the most and Peirson's forces must outnumber them by at least two to one. The French raid had been lunacy from the start. The next hour would see the finish.

The Mont de la Ville was on the left of the Colomberie and two or three hundred yards distant. When the light company of the 95th passed by, going in that direction, Richard resolved to follow them. From the hill, which overlooked the town centre, he would at least be able to see what was happening. Ten minutes later he was on the hill, which the French had apparently made no attempt to occupy. Below him was the Royal Square, with the Town Church to the left and the Royal Court (seen from the back) very much in the centre. The square was held by the French who were formed up facing each entry. They had made little attempt to barricade these entries but they had several cannon in position and manned. The centre of the town was otherwise deserted, shuttered and silent. Below him and to the right some companies of militia had formed up in the Colomberie and La Motte Street, preventing the French escape in that direction. All was quiet for several minutes as the light company of the 95th was taking up position on the hill. They were, of course, far out of range, being posted there merely to complete the surrounding movement. They played no active part in the battle. Then silence was broken by a cannon firing, aimed apparently down Broad Street. All was quiet again until, far off, there came the sound of a drum. It came gradually nearer at a steady pace, inexorable and menacing. Then at last Richard glimpsed the advancing columns, one in Broad Street, the other in King Street. They looked magnificent in scarlet with white crossbelts, with bayonets glittering and swords drawn. The French fired a volley on the word of command and gaps appeared in the marching ranks, only to be filled at once by men from the rear. At last the drum stopped beating and the column in King Street halted, firing a first volley and then resuming their advance. The French replied with a volley and this, at the shorter range, was evi-dently more destructive than their first. The red-coated column wavered for the first time and it looked as if the officer on the right flank had fallen. The troops actually fell back a few paces, firing independently, but the setback was only momentary. The ranks re-formed under command, the advance was resumed and then halted again. Came the crash of another volley and then the sound of cheering as the 95th went in with the bayonet. The French lines broke there and in Broad Street and the enemy fell back, still fighting, into the square. There was a scene of noise and confusion but Richard could see that groups of Frenchmen were throwing down their arms. The firing gradually died away and more redcoats closed in on every side. It was obvious that the battle was over.

The troops on the Mont de la Ville were now given the order to advance and went into the town. Richard followed them and presently found himself in the square where the battle had taken place. The ground was still littered with bodies in the uniform of either side, the wounded were being carried into adjacent houses and the prisoners taken under escort to the Town Church. Richard asked a soldier of the 95th where Major Peirson could be found.

"The Major, sir? He was killed in King Street, sad to tell. He was a brave young officer, none better."

"And Major Corbet?"

"He's over there by the Court House, where the French general fell—the useless, cowardly, rotten fool!" There, sure enough, was a tall and impressive officer, showing his hat to a militia colonel—there had evidently been a bullet through it. This might look well enough, Richard thought, but he would not have been in Corbet's shoes for all that. The man's reputation was beyond repair.

The French weapons were being collected in a heap and Richard added his cutlass to the pile. Having nothing more to do, he walked down to the harbour to ask when the packet for Guernsey would leave. She should have sailed that morning, he was told, but would probably now sail within the hour. He went aboard and paid for his passage, being joined presently by a young ensign from the 78th. His name was Woodcock and he was taking the news to Guernsey of the French defeat.

"By whose orders are you sent?" asked Richard.

"Major Corbet's," said Mr Woodcock. "But, between ourselves, I don't suppose he'll be in command for long. He'll be facing a court martial, I fancy. All the credit will go to Major Peirson, and Corbet is finished. Some of our men fired at him but missed, more's the pity. They hit the French general, though."

"Did they kill him?"

"Not instantly, but he's not expected to live."

"What was the strength of his force?"

"Something over five hundred in St Helier, I'm told. Not all his men landed, it seems, and of those that landed quite a few were drowned."

"With a hundred or so at La Rocque Point, that gives him a total strength of something under a thousand. To attack Jersey with that force seems madness!"

"It was a hazardous enterprise, to be sure. What seems astonishing is that he should so nearly have succeeded."

"He was fortunate to lose so few men as he did in landing. That coast around La Rocque Point is all but impassable; a tangle of rocks, and he attempted it in the dark!"

"He must have had local help—a pilot to lead him in. And someone must have told him that La Rocque Point was unguarded. There was treachery, that's certain."

"There would seem to be no doubt about it."

Richard was glad to have a meal on board the packet after she had sailed. The talk at table was all about the attack on Jersey, several men having their own stories to tell. One had actually seen the Baron de Rullecourt during his brief governorship of the island. Another had known Peter Arrive, a civilian who had been murdered by the French. All agreed that the French had been lucky to succeed as well as they did. Richard agreed silently, thinking to himself that their luck had begun before they landed, for the *Ariel* had missed them by no more than an hour or two.

"Did you hear," one passenger was saying, "of the part played in this affair by a clergyman? He was from St Martin's, I'm told, and he actually brought two guns into action against the French."

"That would be the Rev. M. Le Couteur," said an older man, "I can picture him doing that."

"Yes, that's right. Le Couteur is the name. He comes out of the affair with more credit than most of the soldiers. What went wrong, sir, would you say?"

The question was addressed to Ensign Woodcock, who replied: "Well, to begin with, sir, there was no senior officer on the island."

There was some further discussion about the garrison's lack of vigilance and then the man who had first mentioned Mr Le Couteur came back to that topic.

"A fine man he is, the rector of St Martin's, and my hope is that his part in this affair will always be remembered."

"A fine man he must be," said the ensign. "From what you tell me I would conclude that he should be a bishop."

More to himself than to the others Richard added absently: "Or, anyway, a Canon."

Chapter 10

ALGEÇIRAS

IN NOVEMBER 1781 Richard Delancey joined the *Vernon* storeship at Chatham Dockyard. He had been without regular employment for much of that year but was finally rescued by Captain Henry Trollope, whose acquaintance he had made in America and who was now the commander of the *Kite,* stationed in the Downs. A private letter from Trollope, written in reply to his, advised him that he would find a berth as fourth mate if he applied to the master of the *Vernon.* This recommendation proved effective and Mr Mansell welcomed him aboard. The *Vernon* was no man-of-war but it was soon obvious that she had been taken up for a special purpose. For a mere storeship she was to be unusually well armed and her cargo included a number of gunboats, built in frame and then dismantled and shipped for service overseas. The ship also took on board quantities of provisions and timber, leaving no one with much doubt as to her destination.

"We are bound for Gibraltar, that's certain," said the captain at Richard's first dinner on board. "The French and Spanish must know by now that the place will never be starved into surrender. We have relieved it twice already and they know that we'll do it again. That leaves them with a choice, either to storm the fortress or raise the siege. They'll make their big assault this coming year and I reckon that our gunboats are part of the preparations for beating them off."

"Or will the place fall before we get there?" asked the second mate, Robert Pitman.

"Never!" replied the first mate, Ian Maitland. "General Eliott is not the man to ask for quarter. Did you ever hear tell of him, sir?"

"I don't know that I have," said the captain. "Only that he is governor there and stands well to his guns."

"Well, sir, he knows his trade, having studied fortification in France and Woolwich. He's well over sixty, eats no meat but only vegetables, tastes no wine and sleeps no more than four hours a night. No sentinel of his would dare close an eyelid. He'll hold Gibraltar if anyone can."

"This is how one Scotsman speaks of another."

"He'll hold out, sir—you'll see!"

"We'll see, sure enough, if we come there safely, but I think we shall be under fire. It will be your task, Delancey, to exercise our men at their guns. We are glad to have someone aboard who has served in a king's ship."

"Aye, aye, sir, I'll do my best. But I could wish that our destination were not so generally known. The enemy will hear that we are on the way."

"That's very like. But we'll sail in convoy, mind you, under escort. We'll not be told to run the blockade as a single ship, not with the cargo we have. We'll sail with a fleet."

As the weeks of preparation went by Richard sought to gather news of Gibraltar but without much success. There had been a bombardment and the town, he heard, was in ruins. There had been many casualties from scurvy. The *Brilliant* was there, a frigate commanded by Captain Curtis. There was no news of fighting, though, but only of preparation on either side. Work went on in the *Vernon*, meanwhile, every effort being made to ensure that the gunboats would be easy to reassemble. By January 1782 the loading was finished and the ship made ready for sea. She finally sailed for Spithead where she arrived in mid-February amidst a snowstorm. The captain was then told that the *Vernon* would not be sailing in convoy but would be escorted by the frigate *Success* commanded by Captain Poole. She was also to be joined by Lieutenant-Colonel Gledstanes of the 72nd Regiment and other officers together with a number of recruits. Overcrowding was inevitable but Richard welcomed a plan which would give him more men to man the guns. By the date of sailing from Spithead (11 March) he felt that the *Vernon* was an opponent to be reckoned with. The voyage across the Bay of Biscay was uneventful but there was every likelihood of meeting the enemy in approaching the Straits and there, sure enough, a Spanish frigate was awaiting them, the *San Catalina* (40 guns). The *Success* went to meet her with the *Vernon* in her wake.

So far Richard's main responsibility was for training the gun-crews but he now found that his action station would be on the quarterdeck. Captain Mansell needed his advice. "You stay with me, Mr Delancey, and tell me what the signals mean." No signals were made, in fact, but Richard had some idea of naval tactics and it was he who took the *Vernon* into action. It was a winter afternoon with a threatening sky and a failing light. Seeing the approach of two opponents, the Spaniard went about and shortened sail, allowing the *Success* to draw level on her port beam. Both ships opened fire and maintained the action for nearly half an hour. By then the *Vernon* was able to intervene and Mansell, on Richard's advice, raked the Spaniard with one broadside and then took up a position on her starboard (and windward) beam, engaging her with both cannon and small arms. This was Richard's first experience of a proper naval action and he was surprised to find that he was more interested than frightened. Caught between her two opponents the Spanish frigate was evidently sustaining both damage and casualties. Her fire slackened and her guns still in action were firing too high. One of these brought down the *Vernon's* fore-topsail yard, cluttering the forecastle with broken timber, torn canvas and tangled cordage. Seeing his forward guns out of action, Mansell told Delancey to help the first mate clear the wreckage. Richard ran forward with an axe and had soon freed two of the guns. As he turned with some helpers towards a third he suddenly felt a blow like one from a sledge-hammer. His left arm was numb, his axe had gone and his shirt was soaked in blood. He was only half-conscious when he was carried below and then fainted, luckily being unconscious when the surgeon extracted the musket ball from his upper left arm.

When he came to, perhaps an hour later, Mansell was looking down at him.

"What has happened, sir?" he asked.

"The Spanish frigate has struck her colours. Two other frigates have been sighted and the captured ship is being burnt. We may be in battle again presently but it is dark now and we have to avoid the enemy."

This was the end of the action so far as the *Vernon* was concerned, for the two frigates sighted turned out to be British, the *Cerberus* and *Apollo* escorting four transports. All reached Gibraltar in safety and Richard was among those taken ashore to hospital. Delirious at first and then semi-conscious, Richard was on the danger list for several weeks. When he was well enough to receive a visitor it was Ian Maitland who stood by his bedside, accompanied by Lieutenant-Colonel Gledstanes and his adjutant. As a background to their conversation and to the whole process of Richard's recovery was a distant grumbling of gunfire, lessening at times but never dwindling to silence. Maitland, he realised, was asking him how he did.

"I'm feeling better but still weak," he replied.

"I don't wonder at that," said Maitland. "You lost a lot of blood between the forecastle and the steerage. You are lucky to be alive."

"I'd be luckier, sir, to have escaped the bullet."

"That would have been a miracle," said the colonel.

"Why?"

"Because you were not covered by fire from your own side. The fall of the fore-topsail yard had left the forecastle without a single marksman. One or two had been wounded and the rest were pinned under the wreckage. For ten minutes the opposing enemy marines—those on their forecastle—had mere target practice."

"A painful lesson!"

"You are recovering, though."

"So the surgeon tells me but there is still some pain and irritation. He thought I had tetanus but it seems I haven't. The wound is infected, though, and has hardly begun to heal. But how about the *Vernon?* Are the gunboats put together?"

Richard heard the news on this and on later visits paid to the hospital by his messmates and he soon understood that the *Vernon* was nearly ready to sail on her return voyage. On 5 May Captain Mansell paid a final visit and told him that the ship must sail without him.

"I thought of listing you as a discharged invalid but the surgeon is against it. He thinks you had best remain ashore here and embark for England when recovered. So I have come to say goodbye, and also to thank you for your good services.

The capture of the *San Catalina* was due, in part, to you."

"A pity she was destroyed, sir."

"That was Captain Poole's mistake. He feared that she would be retaken."

"It's very easy to be wise now, sir."

"Very true. There would have been no prize-money for us in any case."

The *Vernon* sailed on the 7th, leaving Richard still in the naval hospital, which overlooked Rosia Bay and was outside the area of the Rock which was actually under fire. When allowed to get up, Richard could see from his window the Bay of Gibraltar with Algeçiras on the far side—the centre, as he knew, of enemy preparations. In the foreground and to his right was the New Mole with the frigate *Brilliant* alongside. At the back of the hospital was the tented camp to which the troops had withdrawn from their damaged barracks at the exposed end of the town. His was a room for three but the other two beds were at first unoccupied, many of the wounded having been sent home to England. Soon after the *Vernon* had sailed, there was brought in Ensign Rogers of the 73rd, crippled by a leg wound but well able to tell Richard about the progress of the siege. The present gunfire was desultory, he explained, and those who had been through the real bombardment were tending to ignore it. That was how he himself had been wounded. The enemy preparations were all centred upon a coming assault to be made, it was said, with shipping.

"I have been watching every day with a spyglass, counting the tents and the ships. They are preparing their big effort for sometime in the summer. The present cannonade is mere routine."

However trivial, the enemy's fire was not wholly ineffective.

A few days later the hospital shook under the impact of a violent explosion and news came that an enemy shell had exploded the magazine of the Princess Anne's battery. As from that time the cannonade intensified but died away again at sunset. In the meanwhile another wounded officer was brought in, this time a naval lieutenant called Moodie of the *Porcupine*. He had been visiting the Princess Anne's battery and had two ribs broken in falling from the level of the platform.

"We were lucky," he said, "that t'other magazine didn't go. It was a damn near thing, I tell you. If the whole of Willis's had gone, the enemy might have risked an attack on the Land Port."

"But what about Princess Anne's battery?" asked Rogers. "Is that out of action, sir?"

"No, the guns are still mounted. They'll open fire as soon as they have powder again, warning the enemy not to try any tricks."

It transpired in conversation that Moodie had been serving with the gunboats, the last of which had been launched on 4 June. Richard asked whether the gunboats were proving of use, confessing his interest as one who had helped bring them out.

"Well, you know, I suppose, what a gunboat is: an oared craft something larger than a ship's longboat and armed with a twenty-four-pounder. Ours each have a crew of 21—eight oars a-side, three men forward and two in the sternsheets. There's a lugsail for use on occasion, the enemy craft having a lateen instead. I have been commanding a division of them numbering five. Given an enemy ship becalmed we might rake her from a position dead aft or forward. But there are more days when we daren't put to sea at all. We'd make a small target in action but could be sunk by a single round. We've done nothing much yet except to scare enemy gunboats, but—who knows?—we might take the enemy battering ships in flank. If we fail, for that matter, we know that the frigates could have done no better and might easily have fared worse."

Richard was discharged from hospital on 17 June and reported at once to Captain Roger Curtis, the senior naval officer.

"So you joined the service in 1775?" said the captain, having heard the story. "You have been at sea for six years or more. Have you passed for lieutenant?"

"No, sir."

"A pity. I'll rate you then as a master's mate, for service with the gunboats. I have a lieutenant who is wounded which leaves me with a temporary vacancy to fill."

Richard entered the *Brilliant's* junior mess with a new sensation of seniority. He was filling a lieutenant's vacancy. He was nearer than he had ever been to commissioned rank. Had he really served the minimum six years? Did his time in the *Vernon* count? But if Captain Curtis thought him eligible, who was he to doubt it? One thing he could not do was to pass his examination. That required three post-captains and Gibraltar—as Richard could see for himself—had exactly two. There was the *Brilliant* and there was the *Porcupine*, two post-ships, and there was the cutter *Speedwell*, a lieutenant's command. There was nothing more and nothing likely to arrive. So Richard plunged into his work with the gunboats and found himself fully occupied in rowing guard under a hot sun. On his second evening aboard the frigate he dined with Captain Curtis and came to know him a little better.

"We are unfortunate," said the captain over his wine, "in being denied the chance of battle at sea. But we must make the most of the opportunities we have. For understanding siege warfare we are well placed indeed and I have come to boast some knowledge of the science. You will find, Mr Delancey, that I encourage my officers to visit the forward posts. We even provided a detachment to take part in the sortie of 27 November— and very well they did, Siward, eh? We have had casualties as a result but have gained in experience. I should hate to feel afterwards that we had merely wasted our time."

Richard took the hint and made friends, when off duty, with Ensign Owen of the 29th and an old engineer officer called Hamilton. Owen, who had taken part in the sortie, was able to point out the line of attack and the parallel which the attackers had destroyed. Hamilton took him over the defensive works and lent him a book in which all the technical terms were explained. What is a demi-bastion, a battery en barbet, a gabion, a half-chandelier, a merlon, a caisson, a fascine, an epaulement, a traverse, a redoubt? All these terms he mastered and memorised. He was also shown the iron gratings which were being added to the northern batteries and on which the shot used could be heated before use. So far no red-hot shot had been fired but the artillerymen were exercised in the drill for using them, the device being reserved for the crisis of the siege. He was surprised to find that the enemy's strength and position was known in the greatest detail, the result of deserters coming over the neutral ground at night. Owen explained, however, that all the fortress's defensive works were as well known to the enemy from men who had deserted to them. The latest news from Spain was that the besieging army was being strengthened by the addition of twenty thousand French troops and that the threatened attack would be launched in September.

Fire from the besiegers' batteries had been dwindling for several days and on the evening of 23 June it ceased altogether and there was a seemingly unnatural and ominous quiet. On the following day Richard was told to report to Captain Curtis. With the captain he found two army officers, the senior of them a member of the governor's staff.

"Good morning, Mr Delancey, I want you to meet Major Palmer and Captain Millington. You will have noticed that the enemy cannon are silent and you may have wondered why. We now learn that the Duc de Crillon has taken command of the allied army, superseding Don Alvarez, and that he plans to attack this fortress from the sea. A number of ships are to be turned into floating batteries, roofed over and strengthened until they are impervious to shot and shell. We are told that work on these ships has begun at Algeçiras and we can see something of this activity from Windmill Hill. We can't approach them in daylight, however, because of the enemy men-of-war. The governor has asked us, therefore, to send a gunboat over at night with the object of reporting on the enemy's progress. I have agreed to do this and have decided to entrust the mission to you."

"Aye, aye, sir."

"Have you any observation to make on what men or equipment you will need?"

"I would suggest taking a smaller boat in tow for use when at close quarters with the enemy. I should like to have the assistance of two good midshipmen and I think that our cannon is needless for this purpose and should be left behind."

"Might not the cannon help cover your retreat?" asked the major.

"We shall be more seaworthy, sir, without that weight in the bows. We are also to be on patrol, in military terms, and what you want from us is intelligence rather than noise."

"Mr Delancey is right," said Captain Curtis. "A military patrol sent on a similar mission would have muskets unloaded."

"I take your point, sir," agreed the major, and the conference ended with a plan accepted in broad outline. More detailed discussion followed the soldiers' departure, and Richard proposed to approach Algeçiras from the westward, passing inside the island. That passage was known to be closed by a boom but Richard argued that a small boat could be hauled over it. The two midshipmen chosen were Jolliffe and Holbrook; the first being steady and reliable, the other an eager youngster with a yearning for action. Concluding his talk to them, Richard ended with these words: "Our success would be complete if we were able to take a prisoner, and a shipwright for choice, one of the men actually working on these ships. I doubt that will be possible but we'll seize any chance that offers."

The night chosen was 24 June, provided only that the weather was calm.

Captain Curtis stood at the entry port as Richard's gunboat, the *Revenge*, was brought alongside the *Brilliant*. Richard reported to him, saying that all was ready. It was midnight when they pushed off, the captain saying "Good luck!" They had about five miles to row over the calm and dark sea.

The muffled oars were plied steadily and the only lights seen were the flares fired occasionally from the Grand Battery and a steady glow from the shipping at Algeçiras on their starboard bow. After pulling for an hour and a half the gunboat approached the land at a point well to the east of Fort San Garcia. Then Richard altered course and steered for the passage behind Algeçiras Island. Two things at once became apparent. First, the workmen on the floating batteries were working at night under a festoon of lanterns. Second, the approaches to the anchorage were well patrolled by guard-boats. Despite the distant noise of hammering, Richard could hear the rhythmic pulse of oars passing between the island and the coast. On his orders the gunboat waited, oars motionless, but the sound ahead of them was continuous and came from at least two boats and more probably three. There was no reason to suppose that the watch was less vigilant on the other side of the island. His original idea had now to be discarded. There was only one alternative and that was to land at the nearest point and walk along the shore until a point was reached from which the floating batteries might be visible.

In a low voice he passed the order to bring the towed boat alongside. Then he gave the following instruction to Midshipman Jolliffe: "I am going ashore here with Mr Holbrook and two seamen, Robins and Gill. Drop the grapnel and wait here in complete silence for two hours. If we have not returned by that time row back to Gibraltar. Is that understood?"

A minute later the two-oared boat was heading for the land, rowed by two picked men. Robins was a big man, immensely strong; Gill, a man who knew a few words of Spanish. All four in the party could swim. Richard brought the boat very slowly and carefully into what proved to be a rocky shore. In any sort of rough sea the boat would have been smashed to pieces but the night was calm and they reached the shore, leaving the boat tied to a rock and marking the place with a handkerchief tied to a stick.

The approach to Algeçiras had to be very cautious indeed. Gill went first, Richard and Robins a few yards behind, and young Holbrook brought up the rear. There was some sort of a path running parallel with the shore and ahead of them were the lights and noises of the harbour. As their advance brought them nearer to the town the danger obviously increased of walking into a sentry post for there could be no doubt that every path would be watched. But neither could much be seen of the ships from any point outside the town frontage. They were moored close together with their sterns towards the beach and they were surrounded by clusters of shore boats. So much was visible but the facts he could so far report were valueless. Bunched as they were, he could not even count them. So the dangerous walk continued, ending abruptly with the sound of a challenge from somewhere ahead of them. There was no shot fired but voices could be heard and footsteps. Richard and Robins left the path silently, followed by Holbrook, and then crawled forward painfully on the seaward side of the track. They could see nothing but it was evident from what they could hear that Gill had been taken prisoner. He would pretend to be a deserter—so much had been arranged beforehand—and would swear that he had come alone. This story was plausible because men usually deserted singly—Richard knew that much without understanding why—and because desertion was fairly common on either side. Without hesitation Richard led the other two towards the shore and presently found himself on a shingle beach near the ruin of what had once been a whitewashed cottage standing a hundred yards back in the direction from which he and his party had come. "We'll leave our weapons here." He whispered, "From this point we shall have to swim." Their pistols, cutlasses, jackets and shoes were hidden and they took to the water without making a sound.

One fact upon which Richard had relied was the relative warmth of the water. Towards the end of a hot summer it was warmer even than the night air. The swim was not exhausting, therefore, but even so Richard planned to go no further than was strictly necessary. He merely went far enough to pass the enemy's picket line, coming ashore when he judged that the sentinels

were behind him. In less than half an hour they were opposite
the nearest of the floating batteries and able to see the others.
There were ten of them, stripped down to the lower masts, and
each was a scene of furious activity. By lantern light a swarm of
men were hammering, shaping, hoisting and jabbering. The
noise was continuous, merging into a sort of murmur but broken sometimes by the higher-pitched screech of the saw. There
were laden barges alongside each of the big ships and oared boats
passing between them and the shore. Part of the total effort was
going into the construction of a steep-pitched roof over each
upper deck, intended no doubt to be bomb-proof and fireproof.
As much effort again was concentrated on a sort of scaffolding
which overhung the nearest ship's port side. If only the one side
were being strengthened it was evident that the ships had only
the one battery and would be defenceless on the starboard side.
This was the first crumb of information he had gained. It might
be important—would be vital indeed to the planning of a gunboat attack—but was quite possibly known already. To discover
anything more would mean making a closer inspection.

"Looks like Noah's Ark, sir," said Robins.

"Fit to sink but not to sail," said Richard's comment.

"Our danger," said Holbrook, "will arise when our gunners
die of laughing."

Richard guessed that time was running short and issued his
orders for the next phase.

"We must have a closer look at the nearest of these monsters.
We shall swim out and hope to find some floating timbers which
will help our return." He led the way down the shingle and into
the sea which seemed colder now than it had been before.

As they swam towards the floating battery they ran the greater
risk of being seen by the light of the lanterns. As against that,

all the men in sight were intent upon their work. There were no sentinels, presumably because of the boom which protected the whole area of preparation. Activity was feverish and Richard guessed that the shipwrights must have been promised some reward for early completion of the task. There were about five hundred yards to go but Richard led the others around the ship's port side, swimming wide of the flat boats which clustered there amidships. Some workmen were swaying up timber from these craft, using a block and tackle. Others were at work on the ship's side adding layer after layer of timber. The total thickness would be ten feet or more. As for the sloping roof, it clearly included layers of old rope and the finished part was being covered with rawhide, identifiable by shape and smell. Forward of the flat boats was a single craft alongside, a xebec with a gig astern and no one visible on deck. Richard swam to her and scrambled on board by means of a trailing rope.

Motioning the other two to hide among the barrels which cumbered her deck, Richard climbed the rigging until he was level with the monster's gun ports, eleven in number. In this part of the ship they were completed, each looking like the entrance to a tunnel. There was just light enough to see that the sides of the tunnels were lined with metal, apparently tin. Back on deck, Richard ascertained that the armouring of the ship was carried down almost to the waterline—would come below the waterline when she was armed and manned. Signalling the others to follow him, he hauled on the gig's painter and slid down into her by the same trailing rope by which he had boarded the xebec. The other two followed suit and Richard cut the painter with his sheathknife. Robins took the oars and Richard pointed the way towards the ship's bows. They passed slowly under her stern and down the other side of the ship, allowing Richard finally to see her name on the stern—*Principe Carlos.* Then it was time to go and Robins pulled for the shore. The boat was undoubtedly seen by several of the workmen but attracted no attention, there being other boats around. By the time it diverged from the others, heading back for the ruined cottage, it was once more in darkness. It was quietly beached and the three of them soon recovered their jackets, shoes and weapons. They walked back along the path, found their own boat, pushed off and duly reached the waiting gunboat.

"We had nearly given you up for lost," said Jolliffe.

"We may all be lost yet," Richard replied, looking at a faint lightening of the sky to the eastwards. "Row now for dear life!"

They were back at the New Mole before daylight.

Richard reported to Captain Curtis soon after his return. After hearing his story the captain said, "Well done. A pity about Gill. Come back at eleven."

When Richard did so he found that Curtis had been joined once more by Major Palmer and Captain Millington.

"Now, Mr Delancey," said the captain, "you need not describe again your actual exploit. Tell us merely what intelligence you have gained."

"I have examined only one of the ten floating batteries, the *Principe Carlos,* with eleven guns on one deck, calibre unknown. She is one of the smaller ships but all appear to have the same sort of bomb-proof protection. The guns forming the ship's port battery are to fire through solid timbers and are sheltered by a sloping roof of timber and junk or possibly cork, covered with rawhide. The gun embrasures are lined with some metal, probably tin. There are no guns mounted on the starboard side, which has no special protection apart from the roof. Work on the *Principe Carlos* is perhaps half completed but other ships are in an earlier stage of preparation. I am no shipwright, sir, but would guess that the floating batteries will not be ready for another eight weeks."

"Thank you, Mr Delancey. Where would you judge these ships to be most vulnerable?"

"From the bows, sir. The forecastle seems to be unfortified."

"Thank you. Gentlemen?" It was clearly Major Palmer's turn and he took it.

"You have given us some facts, clearly stated. I want now to ask your opinion. How effective would you judge these ships to be?"

"They appear to be very formidable, sir, unless engaged on their starboard side. But it seems to me that their fire will be inaccurate."

"Why?"

"Well, sir, when a gun is fired from an ordinary ship the muzzle projects from the port at the instant of firing and the smoke is blown clear by the wind. In these vessels the muzzle will be perhaps eight feet inboard and the smoke will remain in the embrasure. The gunlayers will see nothing after the first round. That is merely an opinion, sir."

"And what gave you that idea?"

"The sheet metal lining the embrasures, sir. The Spaniards realised that the muzzle flash would burn the timber if there were no such protection. That took care of the flash but what could they do about the smoke?"

"What indeed? An interesting point . . . Captain Millington?"

"You mention, Mr Delancey, that the bows seem vulnerable. What about the stern?"

"That was fortified at the level of the gundeck. The rudder is unprotected but is largely under water."

"Any other questions, gentlemen?" asked Captain Curtis. "If not, I'll tell Mr Delancey to get some sleep." There were no other questions and Delancey left the cabin.

"I think you'll agree, gentlemen," said Captain Curtis, "that Mr Delancey has provided us with some valuable information."

"His Excellency will be very satisfied," agreed the major. "Mr Delancey seems to be a useful man."

"I am glad that you think so," said Curtis. "A less resolute officer would have turned back at an early stage in that mission—and with some excuse—but Delancey persisted. I am justified, I think, in making him an acting lieutenant. If His Excellency cares to mention this young officer in his next despatch I should feel confident that the appointment would be confirmed."

"I feel sure, sir, that His Excellency will be glad to do that. We have learnt little more than we knew or suspected about the floating batteries but we now have confirmation of the intelligence we have had from other sources. Mr Delancey's point about the smoke is well taken, however, and will be passed to our artillerymen by way of encouragement."

"I am glad to hear that," said Curtis, rising to mark the end of the conference. "For us Mr Delancey brought more specific information. If our gunboats have the chance to attack they will know—or I will know, rather—how to set about it. And yet, as so often after a mission, I am forced to admit that our only certain advantage is in having tested a young man with a view to his future promotion. In this instance, gentlemen, we must agree, I think, that he has passed the test. I should not hesitate to describe him as a young officer of promise."

Chapter II

Lieutenant

RICHARD was now acting lieutenant, entitled to wear the uniform (but without drawing the pay) of a commissioned officer. A tailor ashore made him a suitable coat and he would have bought a sword had there been one on sale. In the meanwhile he had plenty to do in exercising the gunboats placed under his command. None too sure of himself, he was glad to discover that the seamen viewed him with some respect. He was the youngster who had visited the Spanish ships after dark and was said to have boarded one of them—not a man to trifle with. To clinch his reputation he made a point of visiting the outposts when off duty, listening to the gossip and looking through a spyglass at the Franco-Spanish lines. It was August now and the weather was a great deal hotter than the cannonade on either side. The firing had all but died away, and the soldiers were all confident that the big assault would come in September. While there was little expenditure of ammunition, Algeçiras was the scene of feverish activity. Returning one day from one of these visits to the forward positions, Richard passed the hospital and was surprised to see a naval captain on the point of leaving it. It was not Curtis nor Gibson but a man older than either of them who walked very slowly with the aid of a stick. He was pale and thin, shading his eyes from the sun as if he had been indoors for a long time and was still far from recovered. He returned Richard's salute, smiling faintly, and Richard took the opportunity of asking whether he could be of any assistance. "Can I act as guide, sir, or give you my arm for as far as you mean to go?"

"I need no guide, young man, having known Gibraltar since before you were born, but you can help me as far as that seat over yonder in the shade. This is only my second venture out of hospital and I shan't attempt to go further than that."

It emerged in conversation that the invalid was Captain Bradshaw who had been ill for nearly a year. The physicians had at first despaired of saving his life but he was now convalescent.

"I'm not as young as I was and that's a fact. Still, I seem to be on the mend. How does the siege progress?"

Richard gave him what news he had, sat with the old officer for half an hour and then helped him back to hospital, making conversation as they went.

"So the big assault is to come in a few weeks time, eh?"

"That, sir, is the general belief. The Duc de Crillon must attack soon, for the campaigning season ends in October. If Gibraltar doesn't fall then it won't ever be taken, or so the soldiers say."

"Gibraltar taken? The French and Spanish have as good a chance of reaching the moon!"

Later that day Richard asked permission to see Captain Curtis. He reported to him on board the frigate *Brilliant*.

"I find, sir, that there is another post-captain here; Captain Bradshaw, convalescent in the hospital. That being so, I beg to offer myself as a candidate for promotion, hoping to be examined as soon as Captain Bradshaw is well enough."

"Bradshaw? Yes, I've heard of him and he's high on the list, by George! I'd no idea he was here, though, or I should have done myself the honour of calling on him."

"He has not so far been allowed to receive visitors, sir."

"As ill as that? But now recovering?"

"He tells me, sir, that he is on the mend."

"But how did you come to meet him?"

"We met by chance, sir, near the hospital."

"A stroke of luck, eh? But how did Captain Bradshaw come here in the first place?"

"His ship, the *Hector,* was condemned on survey. He fell sick on passage home in the frigate *Dolphin* and was landed here suffering from what was thought to be a mortal illness."

"The medical men must be pleased."

"Yes, sir—and even more astonished."

"Very well, then, I'll call at the hospital and let you know what I decide . . . Did you hear, by the way, of what happened yesterday at the North Bastion?"

"I was there today, sir. I think the artillerymen were at fault, having too many cartridges near the gun."

"They'll take that lesson with them to the next world. When the big assault comes on the west side that is one of the batteries that will be taken in reverse. It was badly planned in my opinion—and adding the cavalier has made it worse. Our engineers are supposed to know their trade but I wonder sometimes whether some of them are not wanting in experience. No one could say that about General Eliott, I'll allow, but much of the defensive work dates from before his time."

"When did he become governor here, sir?"

"Seven years ago, I understand . . . he is the most extraordinary man I ever met. He is old enough to have fought at Dettingen and Fontenoy—to have been aide-de-camp to King George II. But his energy is astounding! He eats little and no meat at any time, drinks nothing but water and never seems to sleep for more than an hour or two. All this at the age of about sixty-five! Most of what we know about war, Gibson and I, we have learnt from him. An amazing man, the general. I'll contrive some time that you should be presented to him."

"Thank you, sir."

Richard came away from this interview with two impressions, both reassuring. First of all, he was being treated like a brother officer, not like a master's mate filling a temporary vacancy. Captain Curtis seemed almost to assume that he would pass for lieutenant and that his acting-promotion would be confirmed. In the second place, Curtis was so engrossed in siege warfare as almost to see himself as a soldier. Richard began to suspect that he would be examined, at least partly, in engineering, a subject in which he was beginning to feel proficient. What active service he had seen had been mostly ashore! He, too, could almost pass as a soldier. And why not? He was, after all, the great-grandson of a major in Prince Rupert's Regiment of Dragoons. As for the science of fortification, he had best do some revision over the next few days. A week later he was told that his examination would take place on the afternoon of 29 August at the hospital, to which place Captain Bradshaw was still confined.

On the morning of the 28th the enemy's fleet at Algeçiras was reinforced by six Spanish sail of the line. News of this came as something of a shock—the sail when first sighted were thought to be British. With the enemy so strengthened there was nothing further the British frigates could do. Captain Curtis sent for his officers and told them of this change in the situation.

"So you see, gentlemen, we can do nothing against the enemy afloat. This ship and the *Porcupine* will be taken inside the New Mole and probably sunk there. Our other vessels will be similarly withdrawn or beached. All officers and men will march to

a camp at Europa Point, where our sails will provide the mess
tents. We shall there form and exercise as a brigade for service
ashore. I am to rank as colonel and acting brigadier-general, Captain Gibson as lieutenant-colonel. Detailed orders will be issued
later today but I should explain now that eight lieutenants will
rank as army captains, eighteen midshipmen as ensigns. A class
will assemble presently at which Captain Maxwell of the Royal
Marines will repeat and explain the military words of command.
These you should know now but it's easy to forget what we do
not constantly practise. We are all soldiers from tomorrow and
will show the garrison that we are as much to be feared on land
as at sea. That will be all, gentlemen, for the present."

Richard left the captain's day cabin with the others and the
Porcupine's junior lieutenant, Wallis, turned to him with a gri-
mace:

"We shall be nearly dead of fatigue, we soldiers, by tomorrow evening. It will be a day's work not soon to be forgot. But
I hear tell that you have found a way to miss the half of it. A
clever scheme, eh? But I wish you luck."

"Thank you. I am more than a little nervous, though. What
sort of questions must I expect?"

"When I took it, the presiding officer began by saying 'You
command a frigate on the Channel Station and are on passage
from the Downs to Falmouth. There is a freshening gale from
the south, veering to sou'-west and becoming a full gale after
you have passed St Alban's Head at a distance of twelve miles.
It seems doubtful to you whether you can clear Portland Bill.
What orders do you give and to whom?'"

"Easy, so far. I head for Weymouth."

"So did I, but the fore-topmast broke at the cross-trees and
the fore course was blown out of the bolt-ropes."

"And then the rudder fell off, I suppose?"

"That came later, when we were nearly ashore off Kim-meridge."

"So you dropped anchor in ten fathoms and the cable parted a minute later."

"You must have been listening at the keyhole."

"You are lucky to be alive, let alone commissioned."

"At the time I wished I was dead with the ship sunk and the examiners on board."

"But you passed for all that and I hope to God that I can do the same. But Gibson, I hear, is as keen on navigation as Curtis is on seamanship. If one doesn't fail me, t'other will."

"I'll allow that we are all astronomers on board *Porcupine*. How good are you with lunar observations?"

"No good at all. I always add where I ought to subtract."

"Then I'll hope for your sake that Curtis does all the talking. I believe he thinks well of you, anyway."

On the afternoon of the 29th Richard dressed as neatly as possible, borrowed a sword from Tibbenham, third lieutenant of *Brilliant,* and presented himself at the hospital. Ten minutes later an orderly guided him to what was evidently Captain Bradshaw's room on the first floor. Bradshaw must have had a relapse for he was bedridden and looked feverish. Captain Curtis sat at a table under the window with Gibson on his left. There was an empty chair on his right, which Bradshaw might have filled had he been well enough. For official purposes there were, beyond question, three post-captains present. Richard was invited to take a chair facing the presiding officer. He had barely done so when Curtis asked his opening question:

"What is a citadel, Mr Delancey?"

"A fort, sir, with four to six bastions."

"Is Gibraltar a citadel, then?"

"No, sir. It is a fortress."

"And what is a ravelin?"

"A small two-faced work made in the fosse opposite the curtain wall."

"That is correct. Now, you will have seen a stone-built sentry box projecting from the angle of the ramparts. What is it called?"

"An echangette, sir; or possibly a guerite."

"Just so. You will no doubt have noticed that the Spanish cannon we had facing the Neutral Ground were recently replaced by British ordnance of smaller calibre, the Spanish guns being now mounted in the batteries which face the Bay. Why do you suppose that His Excellency the Governor should have issued orders to that effect?"

"Our Spanish guns are twenty-six-pounders, sir, and the enemy cannon they were formerly engaging were of the same calibre. Our shot could therefore be used again by the Spanish artillerymen. With the ordnance exchange, the shot fired at the Spanish lines will be useless to the enemy, being of the calibres we use, eighteen and twenty-four-pounders, while our twenty-six-pounder shot, fired at their ships, will never be recovered from the sea. Shot of this calibre, however, fired at our lines flanking the Landport, can easily be taken to Montague's or Orange's Bastion and used again against their floating batteries."

"Exactly! Now, I realise that you were not here when the sortie was made in November last year. You will have heard of its success, however, and of the destruction which resulted of the enemy's second parallel. Should we be justified in making such another sortie now?"

"No, sir. It would do nothing to spoil their main attack which we expect to come by sea. It would also result in heavy casualties on either side; and whereas the enemy could replace his losses we could not replace ours and so would have the worst of the bargain."

"Agreed. Captain Gibson?"

Richard expected a dramatic change in the type of questions asked but Gibson in turn seemed to be every inch a soldier.

"What is meant by Flanc Rasant?"

"The fire directed from one bastion so as to pass the face of an adjacent bastion and so enfilade any force which may attempt the assault."

"Correct. Captain Curtis reminded you just now of the sortie which took place last year. It was accompanied, though not led, by the governor himself. Was he justified in taking such a risk?"

"His taking it was perhaps unusual, sir, but I have learnt to avoid comment on the decisions made by so senior an officer."

"Eh? . . . Quite so, quite so. I have no further questions to ask, sir." Captain Gibson looked somewhat put out and Captain Curtis smiled faintly before walking over to Captain Bradshaw's bedside.

"Have *you* any questions to ask, Captain?" It would seem that Bradshaw had been half asleep but he roused himself with an effort.

"Question? Question? Yes, I have *one* question to ask, dammit. When will this confounded noise stop?" A distant rumble of gunfire was heard, lending point to the invalid's query.

"When the main assault has failed, sir," said Richard, "in a week or ten days' time."

It is doubtful whether Bradshaw even heard the reply but Curtis came briskly back to the table, sat down, and looked at

Gibson with an inquiring glance. Gibson nodded and Curtis concluded the examination.

"I am glad to tell you, Mr Delancey, that you have passed and that you have the rank of lieutenant, subject to Admiralty confirmation. I return you your logbooks and testimonial letters, which are all very creditable. You will serve as my aide-de-camp for the time being but will return to the gunboats if and when we have the opportunity to use them. My congratulations, Mr Delancey, and good day to you." Curtis began writing his letter of recommendation and Richard, saluting, left the room and made his way to the Europa Camp.

The scene there was one of tremendous activity. Processions of heavily laden men were bringing stores and hammocks from the quayside. Others were manhandling the cannon that had been brought ashore and others again were rigging up tents made from the frigates' sails. Hot as it was, the seamen were all very cheerful, perhaps because of a break in the monotony of life afloat. They were inclined to skylark when out of the boatswain's sight but the work was being done and the camp was taking shape. The batteries round the tip of Gibraltar faced west and south and were being hurriedly extended so that additional guns could be mounted. The wardroom had been established on the inland side of the camp and there Richard found Peter Wallis of the *Porcupine,* tired and thirsty. In answer to a question, Richard said that he had passed.

"Congratulations, Mr Delancey! I drink your health and later this afternoon, I should warn you, your messmates will expect to do the same."

"The wine is on the way—I sent my servant to fetch it—but it won't be champagne and we shall be lucky if it's even drinkable. I had a choice between some nameless wine from Malaga which might pass as claret and some cloudy-looking white stuff which had probably gone bad. I chose the red as the better of the two."

"You chose wisely. I had some of that white ullage the other day and was sick afterwards. They serve it at the gunners' mess and it looks and tastes like turpentine. What I would give for just one decent meal!"

There was nothing memorable about their dinner when it came. Months had passed since the last provision ship had run the blockade and even boats from the African shore were few and small with cargoes absurdly overpriced. Richard wet his commission, though, and was afterwards made to sing a song. His choice was a hymn which normally begins with the words "Ye watchers and ye holy ones" but the words of which were amended as follows:

Orderly officer ev'ry day

This is all I ever have to say:

"Put those lights out! Put those lights out!

"Put those lights out! *Put those lights out!*

"PUT THOSE LIGHTS OUT!"

Other hymns, it was found, had a vaguely military theme and phrases about "soldiers of Christ" lent themselves to parody. Richard could have been very funny about his examination in siege warfare but decided, very wisely, to keep quiet about it. There were several army guests present and Richard escorted one of them to the camp entrance after the party had broken up. Captain Pritchard of the 58th was a thoughtful young man whose opinion was evidently worth having. Richard asked him when the big assault was to be expected.

"Not until the enemy fleet arrives from Cadiz. We have that from a deserter who came in the day before yesterday."

"Are deserters to be trusted?"

"We think this one is. He came from Minorca, you see, and was taken prisoner there when the island fell. He was known to some of our men. Besides that, his report seems to make sense. Without their fleet they would be outnumbered, gun for gun, by the batteries they are to engage."

"So what is the date to be?"

"On the 15th, as I should guess. They dare not leave it any later for fear the weather might break. But they have still to roof in the last of their floating batteries, for which I'll allow ten days. Add a day or two for final preparations and for embarking troops and we find that the 15th is the earliest day as well as the latest."

"My hope is that you are right. That will give us time to train our Naval Brigade."

"Do you need training? Your seamen are all artillerymen already."

"Yes, but our brigadier-general wants them to serve equally well as infantry, ready to attack the enemy if they land."

"Does he, egad? You'll be working hard!"

This last prediction fell short of the truth. The work was all but killing. The trouble at first was that watching soldiers would jeer and snigger. When these had been ordered away the seamen would laugh at their own mistakes, unable to take the platoon drill seriously. Each exercise presupposed that the enemy had landed, capturing the Europa batteries. It was for the Naval Brigade to counter-attack and recapture the lost ground by coordinated fire and movement. Each day the mock battle ended in confusion, leaving Richard more exhausted than anyone else. One initial difficulty arose from the fact that the seamen, familiar with the boatswain's pipe, were ignorant of the bugle calls.

It was the task, therefore, of Curtis's A.D.C. to run backwards and forwards, conveying orders, counter-orders, explanations and reproof. The September sun was warm even in the early morning and Richard was tired out long before the final bugle call ended the battle. Added to his physical exhaustion was a sneaking suspicion that the exercise was futile. His own belief was that the great assault would begin and end with an artillery duel. If the defenders won this, the infantry attack would never develop. If they lost it, the fortress would be untenable and the British would be overwhelmed by sheer weight of numbers. If it came to a pitched battle, the allies could throw forty thousand men against a garrison which numbered about seven thousand at most. Such an action should be over within the hour. In numbers of cannon the odds were more nearly even and the guns of the fortress were better placed in more permanent fortifications.

The Europa batteries were first in action on 9 September when nine of the enemy warships sailed across the bay and bombarded the position as they passed. Then they tacked and fired their other broadsides as they headed back to their anchorage. Standing beside Captain Curtis and Lieutenant-Colonel Fraser of the 58th, Richard observed the effect of the fire and reported what he had seen, shouting to make himself heard. The sound of gunfire from the north and west side of the Rock was now a continuous rumble. Captain Gibson asked his senior officer what the enemy were trying to do. Curtis repeated the question to Lieutenant-Colonel Fraser, deferring to that soldier's greater knowledge.

"They are drawing our fire," Fraser explained patiently. "They have only a rough idea of our effective strength. How many men have we on the sick-list? Can we man all our batteries at the same time? Today they have opened fire from the land, sent in their gunboats along the sea front and engaged us here with their men-of-war. Their fire has been returned at every point; which it would not have been, by the way, if your Naval Brigade had not been formed. They will make their plan accordingly."

"So they won't attack today?"

"No, sir."

"But what they have learnt this morning, that will influence their plan?"

"They know now that a feint attack would be a waste of effort. As all our batteries are manned no threat at one point will weaken any other. Their main effort, sir, will be their first."

"What will they do next, then?"

"I suspect, sir, that they will repeat this last exercise but after dark, drawing our fire under different conditions. They may not have decided yet on a day or night attack."

"What if we held our fire, Colonel?"

"They would conclude, sir, that we are short of ammunition. I would rather discourage them with the idea that we are short of nothing."

Lieutenant-Colonel Fraser's prediction was borne out by the events which followed. There was a fresh cannonade in the small hours of the following morning, fire being drawn from all the batteries at the same time, the same ships passing and repassing Europa Point. For an hour or two the night was lit with the flash of the guns. Then the firing died away, a few cannon firing in the distance at a lengthening interval until all was quiet again save for the barking of dogs and the tramp of the gunners marching back to camp. Other parties were replenishing the ammunition and removing the wounded.

"Tomorrow, Colonel—or the next day?" asked Curtis.

"Not tomorrow, sir. They have not yet destroyed our palisades.

There can be no general assault until those are breached."

Fraser and his adjutant went back to his regiment's lines, immediately to the right of the Naval Brigade. Outside his tent Curtis said good night to his staff. As Richard saluted and turned away there was a further rumble of gunfire in the distance, followed again by an uneasy silence. The day after tomorrow—the day after that? It could not be long now.

Chapter 12

ARMAGEDDON

THE STAGE was set for battle on 12 September. In the morning a fleet was seen approaching from the westward. There were doubts at first whether the men-of-war were French or British but they were soon recognised as the combined fleets of France and Spain; 38 sail of the line including three-decked ships and accompanied by smaller craft. Joined to the nine already there, the fleet numbered 47, added to which were the ten floating batteries and a swarm of landing craft. That afternoon began the destruction of the palisades, the essential preliminary to an infantry assault from the land. That evening Captain Curtis called his officers together in the wardroom tent and told them to expect the main attack that night.

"This afternoon, gentlemen, I was in conference with His Excellency and the other senior officers. Our conclusion was that the enemy will assault soon after midnight. Their first object will be to place their floating batteries in position opposite the King's Bastion. If we have correctly interpreted their attempts to take soundings we may expect them to choose a range of a thousand yards. They will hope to reach their chosen anchorage under cover of darkness. It will be their intention to assault the Land-port at the same time and perhaps Europa Point as well. From all our intelligence sources we learn that the enemy have put their trust in their floating batteries. It is said that they will commit no other ships during the first phase of the battle. Should that be their plan and should our batteries here be left without a target, I may be able to bring our gunboats into action. In the meanwhile, our batteries will be manned as from the sounding of the last post but with permission for the men to sleep beside the guns. Those acting as infantry can sleep in camp but must be ready to march in five minutes after the alarm is sounded. That is all, gentlemen. Take some rest while you can."

There was no attack that night and Richard won a small bet on it. The French, he argued, would never assault in darkness, not with the Comte d'Artois and the Duc de Bourbon there to witness the action. Daybreak would be the time and so it proved to be. The whole garrison stood to their posts and the morning light showed the battering ships under way, heading for Gibraltar, leaving the combined fleet at its moorings and out of range. The defending batteries held their fire until the battering ships were in position but as from the moment the first enemy ship dropped anchor all hell broke loose on land and sea. With about four hundred guns in action, the noise was indescribable.

"Damnation!" shouted Captain Curtis, above the uproar. "They are not coming near us. We are mere bystanders, dammit."

This was the sad truth, for the ten floating batteries were far to the north, the nearest of them engaging the King's Bastion and the furthest in action against the Old Mole. The staff of the Naval Brigade were gathered at a point from which they could see but that was all they could do. The scene before them, however, was stupendous. It was a sunny day with excellent visibility and they were awestruck by the sheer immensity of the forces collected for the assault. The Spanish tents seemed to cover the mainland, the allied shipping filled the bay with a forest of masts and rigging, troops in thousands were ready to embark in hundreds of landing craft and tens of thousands more were grouped beyond the enemy parallels, formed up to assault when the defending batteries had been silenced. The display of strength seemed incredible and none who gazed had any illusions about the allied leadership. The Duc de Crillon was a distinguished general, the Chevalier D'Arçon a leading engineer, Don Moreau a flag officer of great experience and courage. That the attack would be pressed home was certain. As for the floating batteries, now half hidden in smoke, they might seem clumsy, each with a jury rig poking through its Noah's Ark roof, but they could yet prove to be as invulnerable as they were meant to be. It was the fact, nevertheless, that they were fighting at a disadvantage. The defending artillerymen had a ship to fire at, its position marked by its topmasts. The gunners in the floating batteries had to fire at embrasures in the solid stonework; embrasures which would be invisible after the first broadside. And, apart from that, how were they to aim? A gun firing through a ten-foot tunnel could hardly traverse. Elevate they could—it looked, indeed, as if they were firing too high—but no embrasure would be hit without the merest fluke. With firing on the present scale the garrison would suffer casualties, no doubt, but not as a result of aimed shots. The British batteries, Richard told himself, could never be silenced by a merely random fire. Was he, however, confusing hope with belief? He would know, and so would everyone else, by the time night fell.

The bombardment continued as the day wore on, neither side seeming to have the advantage. But stalemate, in this instance, meant defeat for the allies. If they could not overpower the defending artillery their infantry dared not attack and Gibraltar would never fall. So the bombardment continued, the defenders presently loading with red-hot shot after observing that cold shot made no impression on the battering ships. It was not until the

afternoon that the enemy's fire began to slacken. In the meanwhile Captain Curtis was all but dying of frustration, his guns
silent and his men at ease. Before midday he sent the governor
a message offering to relieve the artillerymen who had been
most hotly engaged. A rather curt reply told him to watch his
own front, which the enemy might still choose to attack. In the
early afternoon Curtis had another idea, to attack the floating
batteries with gunboats. He was about to put this proposal into
writing but changed his mind and told Richard to deliver a
verbal message.

"You will find His Excellency at the King's Bastion. Give him
my compliments and my submission that the southernmost battering ships might be raked from the bows. We can still man the
Europa batteries after making this detachment. You are familiar
with the gunboats and can answer any question he may ask
about their capabilities."

"Aye, aye, sir."

"Take your servant with you, as orderly, Mr Delancey, and
report back to me here."

Richard collected his orderly, a youngster called Bob Hewitt,
and set off to walk a distance of over two miles. He followed the
path which led behind the South Barracks, leaving the main
infantry camp on his right, passing Rosia Bay and heading for
the New Mole. He had decided to make certain that the gunboats were unharmed before he delivered his message. Had they
been destroyed—which was unlikely but just possible—Curtis
would be made to look a fool with his proposal for deploying
resources which did not exist. Richard ran up to the rampart
and saw that the gunboats were unharmed. The guns here were
in action but those further on, opposite the Princess of Wales's
Lines, were mostly silent, unable to bear on the target. Then he

hurried on, the noise of the bombardment intensifying as he came near the Ragged Staff. At this point he entered the town of Gibraltar by the South Port. There were storehouses, little damaged, on his right, the governor's residence on his left, the Spanish Church ahead of him. The area he was entering was very much under fire, with buildings already destroyed and shot passing overhead. Turning left beyond the Spanish Church, he headed for the King's Bastion, beyond which the whole town lay in ruins. He slowed down at this moment, resolved to avoid being out of breath when he delivered his message. As momentarily representing the Royal Navy he must seem calm and collected. A damaged building on his left was hit by another shot and mostly collapsed in a cloud of brick-dust.

"Strewth, sir," yelled Hewitt, "it's like the end of the world!"

Approaching the rear of the King's Bastion was more like a descent into hell. There were here a row of furnaces kept red-hot by the bellows and served by sweating and dirt-caked men, stripped to the waist and gasping for breath. The cannon balls were being shovelled out and placed on iron gratings or wheel-barrows half-filled with sand. Parties of weary men were hurrying the projectiles towards the cannon. Keeping to windward of these, Richard entered the King's Bastion as the cannon fired. It was not a volley at word of command but a scattered series followed by a pause of a minute or two while the guns were reloaded. At first Richard could see nothing at all for the smoke had blown back through the embrasures. Then the smoke cleared and Richard realised that the south-westerly breeze had stiffened. A glance at the sea told him that the waves were flecked with white. Overhead the union flag was fluttering and straining towards the Rock, a proof that the wind direction was unchanged. In frantic motion round the guns were the artillerymen, their faces and arms blackened with powder, the sweat pouring off them and fatigue already obvious. The subalterns and non-commissioned officers were striving to keep up the rapidity of fire without loss of accuracy and danger of mishap. In rear of the cannon, with their backs to Richard, were grouped some senior officers, with orderlies and buglers still further to the rear. "That is where the governor will be," Richard told himself. The cannon thundered again and blotted out the entire scene. As the smoke cleared Richard stepped forward and reported to a junior staff officer on the near fringe of the group. "A message for His Excellency from Brigadier-General Curtis." The junior officer reported in turn to one more senior, who finally spoke to the chief of staff. At a gesture from the latter officer, Richard stepped forward on the governor's left and removed his hat with a flourish. "Lieutenant Delancey, Your Excellency, aide-de-camp to Brigadier-General Curtis." At that instant the cannon volleyed again, hiding the whole Bastion in smoke. Richard felt rather foolish, making his best bow towards someone he couldn't even see, but he stayed in position until the smoke cleared. The central figure then returned his salute casually and said "Well?" Having rehearsed his lines over the last half hour, Richard spoke without hesitation:

"Brigadier-General Curtis sends his compliments and begs to submit that his gunboats might do good service on the enemy's right flank, enfilading their line at a fairly close range."

The general, an impressive figure in scarlet, black and gold, did not even look at Delancey. He first looked through his telescope at the enemy men-of-war, to see whether they were still at anchor. Seeing that they were, he glanced at the sea and upwards at the flag, looking finally towards the New Mole. When he spoke it was very deliberately:

"Have the gunboats sustained any damage?"

"No, sir."

"Has the wind freshened since you left the Europa Lines?"

"Yes, sir."

"Would you agree that the sea is now too rough?"

"Yes, sir. But it may moderate before nightfall."

"Or so you hope. What is your name?—I failed to catch it."

"Delancey, sir."

"Delancey . . . Are you the young officer who reconnoitred these battering ships?"

"Yes, sir."

"I thought I remembered . . . What do you think of them?"

"They can aim a broadside, sir, but they cannot aim a gun."

"As you reported, and I think correctly. Very well, then. My compliments to Brigadier-General Curtis and he is ordered to bring the gunboats into action if and when the weather moderates. He will be responsible—" The guns fired again, the smoke blowing back over the platform. When it cleared General Eliott continued calmly:

"He will be responsible for preventing his gunboats masking the fire from the batteries. Is that clear?"

"Yes, sir."

Richard looked for a moment into the general's face, austere, sad and desperately tired. The expression changed suddenly. With a brief smile the general ended the interview on a note of curt dismissal.

"Give them hell when you have the chance! Off with you!"

Richard stepped back, doffed his hat again, turned and hurried off. So far from giving the enemy hell he seemed at that moment to have entered hell himself. He was to leeward of a hot-shot grating, the heat from which swept over him with deadly effect. He stumbled on, sweating and trembling, and then the guns roared again and he was lost once more in the smoke. He somehow found himself back at the Spanish Church with Hewitt still at his heels. He made for the South Port, feeling vaguely that the situation had changed for the worse. For some unexplained reason the enemy fire was extending further south. A shot passed overhead as he crossed the Red Sands, ploughing into the hillside above him. Remembering that the floating batteries were anchored bow and stern, he guessed that one of them, perhaps the southernmost or leading ship, had lost her forward cable, hit by a chance shot. She would have swung on her stern anchor, head to wind, her guns on a south-easterly bearing. It went to prove his contention that the enemy could aim a broadside but could not traverse a gun. He felt oddly pleased about this, aware as he was of the fire now coming in his direction.

His route back was slightly different from the way he had come; further from the New Mole, which he had no occasion to visit again, and nearer to the Naval Hospital. Shots were still coming his way and he saw some of them crash into the hospital itself. Passing the entrance, he saw an orderly run out, probably to ask for help, and called to him "Anyone hurt?" The orderly paused just long enough to reply "Captain Bradshaw has fallen, sir," and went on towards the infantry lines. So the old officer had been killed in his bed after all, the victim of an unintentional shot from some smoke-blinded gunner. He had survived just long enough for Richard's purpose . . . Putting that thought on one side, Richard hurried on and reached Europa Camp at a quarter past two. Making his report to Captain Curtis, he ended with the governor's words, "Give them hell when you have the chance!"

Glancing seawards, Curtis decided that his chance had come.

"The wind is more moderate now. All gunboat crews to the New Mole! Collect your men, gunboat commanders, and be ready to sail at half past three. Pass the word for the gunboat officers! At the double—move!"

By a forced march the gunboat crews were on board and ready to cast off at the time laid down. Near where they were stationed Captain Curtis had his telescope to his eye and was examining the enemy ships with close attention. He came to the conclusion that the flagship was on fire, as was also the ship next astern. Others had lost their masts and rigging and nearly all had been considerably damaged. It remained to finish them off, and Curtis promptly decided to lead the gunboats in person, making one of them (not in Richard's division) the "flagship," distinguished by an ensign. There were three divisions, each of five boats, Lieutenant Wallis commanding the first, Lieutenant Tibbenham commanding the second and Delancey commanding the third. Hoisting their lugsails, they sailed in that order, each division in line abreast, Curtis himself being with Tibbenham. The cannonade still continued but the fire from the floating batteries was plainly slackening. Signals were being made, evidently asking for assistance, and boats were seen approaching from the allied fleet, presumably to rescue the crews of ships that were on fire. As the floating batteries had not surrendered, Wallis's immediate task was to drop his sails and open fire on these boats, which were also under fire from the shore. Tibbenham's division was directed by Curtis to open fire on the leading enemy ship, keeping directly ahead of her, and Delancey's division was held in reserve, ready to exploit any opportunity that might offer. The situation was one in which gunboats had an almost unique chance of proving useful.

The gunboats slowly closed the range, bows-on to the enemy

ships, Wallis's guns firing at the rescue boats which were soon forced to withdraw. To have ordered the other boats into action, widening the line abreast, would have brought the flanking boats into the enemy's arc of fire. Smoke was pouring from the ships in the centre of the enemy line but those nearest were still firing and each had at least two guns which could almost be brought to bear.

"A pity, sir, that we can't let them do their own rescue work," said Delancey's coxswain.

"It is a pity, I must confess," said Richard, "but we don't know that their boats wouldn't bring more men to put the fire out. And those they rescue can fight again tomorrow."

"If there's any fight left in 'em!"

The coxswain assumed that the battle had been won but Richard was not as sure. Having seen the shore batteries in action at the King's Bastion, he found it almost unbelievable that their fire could be sustained. They were still firing steadily hours after the gunners might have been expected to collapse in utter exhaustion. What they were doing did not seem humanly possible. As for the floating batteries, their fire had slackened but there was nothing (save the gunboats) to prevent the enemy from replacing their gun-crews after dark. Granted that several of them were now doomed to destruction, the others could, in theory, resume the battle at daybreak. If they ever had this intention it broke down over the central fact that the British cannonade went on. The only very minor respite was caused by Wallis's gunboats exhausting their ammunition. Their place was taken by Tibbenham's division and Curtis sent Wallis's gunboats back to the New Mole to replenish their powder and shot. By the time Delancey's division was signalled into action Richard found to his surprise that it was already half past four. The boats rowed

forward in line, passing through Tibbenham's boats as they withdrew. As they did so, Captain Curtis waved him to come
alongside. A minute later Curtis was on board Richard's gunboat,
bringing with him a midshipman and his orderly, the last carrying a flagstaff and ensign. As soon as the ensign was hoisted
Curtis said to Richard "You are flag captain now! Order your
other boats to close in on us." When they were collected, Curtis addressed them briefly, shouting to make himself heard above
the gunfire:

"Listen, men. You can't be in action long because our ammunition is limited. So every shot must take effect. We have nothing
to throw away. We can't sink these floating timber yards but we
can do two things. We can prevent the enemy from putting more
men aboard them and we can hinder them in their efforts to put
out each fire. Use round shot against any boat you see. Use
grapeshot against the roofs or wherever you see smoke. The governor's orders are to give them hell. So do just that!"

Richard restored his formation, line abreast, and signalled
them to open fire in turn from the right. The "flagship" was then
the third to fire, its 24-pounder jarring the whole boat along the
line of the keel. The smoke drifted forward concealing what
effect, if any, had been gained. Glancing to starboard, Richard
received a signal from his Number Two boat indicating a reduced
elevation. When Number Four boat fired in turn, Richard
watched the result and signalled a correction in his turn.

"Is this *your* system, Mr Delancey?" Curtis asked.

"Yes, sir. I hope you approve, sir. It's impossible, in practice,
to observe the fall of your own shot but we can observe for each
other as long as we fire in order."

"I can see that. But aren't you slowing down the rate of fire?"

"We should do that, sir, if there were more than five boats

in line. With this number we reckon to *improve* the rate a little. Each boat must reload before its turn comes again. If any boat's crew is slow the others notice it and make game of them afterwards. They hate the derision of their shipmates more than any reproof from me."

"You have something there, Mr Delancey. Now show me how you cease fire."

The cannon thundered once more, jarring the boat, and the coxswain, at a nod from Richard, held an oar upright with a black and white rag attached. The guns fired from boats Number Four and Five and then the firing stopped.

"A new target, Mr Delancey, on the port bow!" Richard cursed under his breath for there, sure enough, were two launches nearing the second of the floating batteries. If he had not been explaining his drill, he would have seen them a few seconds sooner. Grabbing the oar from the coxswain he swung it twice to his left and pointed. Then he held it vertically for a moment. As he brought it down again the gun boomed from Number One gunboat. The first three shots missed but Number Four scored a hit and so did Number Three at the second try. Both launches showed the white flag of surrender and Curtis ordered the division to advance. Within a few minutes the captured launches were on their way to Ragged Staff under escort of Number One.

Having learnt from the prisoners that there were some men still aboard one of the burning ships, Curtis sent Number Five to rescue them. As this was being done there came a deafening explosion from the far end of the enemy line. The fire had spread to the magazine of one of the battering ships. This suggested a new danger to Richard, quite apart from the fire of their own friends ashore, but Curtis was working off his earlier frustration. He was longing to capture one of the enemy ships by boarding and pushed on with that object in view. When he was nearly opposite the centre of the enemy line, however, there was another tremendous explosion. One of the centre ships had blown up with a noise like the crack of doom. The noise was so shattering that the gunboat officers did not immediately realise their danger. With the roof blown sky-high, the broken timbers, some of them burning, began to rain down over the vicinity of the disaster. Avoiding action was impossible for the fragments appeared from nowhere through the smoke to plunge, hissing, into the sea. These deadly missiles were falling everywhere in quick succession. Everyone waited and watched for what seemed an eternity. Then, with dreadful suddenness, a blazing beam fell like a meteorite, lanced through the bottom of gunboat Number Four and sank the vessel in a matter of seconds. Most of her crew were rescued by Number Two and Curtis directed Richard to steer for the same spot. A minute later the "flagship" (Number Three) was hit by another thunderbolt which crashed through the sternsheets. It so happened that Curtis and Richard had both moved to the bows, looking out for survivors from Number Four, but for which circumstance they would have perished. As it was, the coxswain was killed outright and the man at the stroke oar was badly wounded. The gunboat itself would have sunk but two seamen stuffed their jackets into the hole. With only two undamaged gunboats under command, Curtis signalled his flotilla out of action. They began a limping withdrawal towards the New Mole.

It was evening now, the smoke hastening the approach of darkness. The Spanish admiral might have hoped to withdraw at least some of his ships but they were all now alight, those least damaged having received the burning debris from those that had blown up. No one vessel had the means of making sail and few had so much as a mast standing. Worst of all, the light from those actually ablaze was illuminating the rest, making them perfect targets, brightly outlined against the darkness of the sea. Surprisingly enough, they were still under heavy fire from the shore batteries, which apparently had a new lease of life. It would seem that these astounding gunners were ready to continue the action indefinitely. They had been told to give the enemy hell and it was to hell that many of the Spanish were now consigned, left to choose whether they would burn or drown. Looking about him, Richard thought of battle paintings he had seen, pictures of men-of-war in strict formation under a blue sky with white smoke from their broadsides and cloud shadows on the green-grey sea. Real war, he realised, is not like that. This was the real thing: the glare and crackle of the flames, the debris in the sea, the screams of agony, the wrecked ships lit by those ablaze, the whole scene of chaos which no artist could ever record. One thing clear was that the victory had been won. There was no fight left in the floating batteries, no possibility that the attack would be renewed. They passed three ships in slow succession, each in flames and apparently abandoned. Coming near the fourth, Captain Curtis became aware that it was on fire but with part of the crew still on board. He led his surviving gunboats in that direction, telling his men to rescue as many survivors as they could.

At this stage of his career Richard was a young man of merely average courage, braver on some days than others. He had so far done what he had to do and sometimes more than was strictly necessary. It cannot be said, however, that he would run into danger for the fun of it. And by this last order he was frankly appalled. These enemy ships were going to explode, one by one, just as soon as the flames reached their magazines. Any gunboat near them when this happened would be inevitably destroyed. His own leaking gunboat had been within an ace of destruction and could only be kept afloat by continual baling. All common sense suggested a prudent withdrawal but his luck was out. His commanding officer was a hero assigned for most of the day to an unheroic role. Given half a chance he had plunged into battle after the victory had been won. Still dissatisfied he had now to prove himself another Galahad. The trouble with Curtis, Richard told himself, was that the man wanted his knighthood before the war ended. He assumed that there would be no other war in his lifetime. What was the loss of three gunboats as compared with this last chance of distinction? Forgetting for the moment that his own confirmation as lieutenant might depend on this same throw of the dice, he raged inwardly at the risk he was having to take. It was, after all, the duty of a brigadier-general to command his brigade, not to play knight errant at the head of a mere detachment. Then he remembered his own priggish answer to Captain Gibson . . . Perhaps Curtis was right after all. He had certainly been the first to see those enemy launches. Damn and blast the whole situation! Why couldn't he have been left to command his own division in his own way?

Curtis actually visited two enemy ships, the foremost of their line; and saved as many men as his gunboats could embark. A far greater number were unavoidably left to their fate. At this stage Curtis was hoping to save more when his other gunboats returned. They did not reappear, however, and there was nothing more he could do. The overladen boats made a slow passage back to the New Mole. On the way Captain Curtis was suddenly communicative.

"Some people would say that I was wrong to go with the gunboats, that I should have sent Gibson instead. For a whole lot of reasons that would have been a mistake. Some people again—and I think you might be among them—would question whether I should have stayed to rescue these wretched Spaniards. You won't see it until you are older but that *had* to be done. Some other officer in my place would have thought it too great a risk but he would, I know, have been in error. It was, you see, a calculated risk—" (There was at that moment another tremendous explosion but the gunboats were clear by now of the danger area.) "Yes, we had time enough—not *too* much time, I grant you—but time enough. Our garrison will be here, you see, after the war is over. The Spanish are folk we shall have to live with. So their wounded are going to receive the best possible care. The Spaniards should find that we are good friends and neighbours but that we are the last people in the world to have as enemies."

When Captain Curtis landed at the New Mole, with Delancey at his side, he was met on the quayside by Captain Gibson.

"In your absence, sir, I received a message from His Excellency directing that a hundred of our men should relieve the artillerymen on the batteries principally engaged. I sent them off under the command of Mr Trentham. When the gunboats returned with Mr Wallis and Mr Tibbenham I ordered them on the same service. I hope you will approve, sir. I have manned alternate guns in the Europa batteries and propose to relieve Mr Trentham's detachment at midnight."

"Your arrangements are approved, Captain Gibson. Mr Delancey, march your detachment back to camp. They can rest now but will be on duty again at midnight. The prisoners and wounded will remain here with Captain Gibson, who will dispose of them. You will be responsible, Mr Delancey, for sending all carpenters from the camp to repair the gunboats, which should be serviceable by daybreak. Boatswain, check the stores here and let me know what we shall need to replace damaged oars, sails and cordage. Gunner, see that the gunboats' ammunition is replaced before daybreak. Surgeon, I shall want a report on the wounded as soon as they are in hospital. Master-at-Arms . . ."

Richard went off with his detachment, leaving the captain with a night's work ahead of him. He had envied senior officers in the past but he was beginning to see that Curtis had to earn far more than he was ever likely to be paid. He had still to think and plan and organise even when completely exhausted. Perhaps he deserved that knighthood after all.

Richard was on duty again at midnight, as ordered, his detachment of seamen manning guns at Europa Point while those previously posted there were marched down to the King's Bastion.

The firing of the shore batteries continued all night, punctuated at intervals by the explosion of the floating batteries. There were only two left at first light, both abandoned and neither worth repairing. It was only gradually, however, that the garrison came to realise that the siege was over, the battle won. The allied army remained in position and the blockade was to continue for months with a daily cannonade as if to preface some new assault. But the heart had gone out of the siege. What finally ended the Spanish dream of taking Gibraltar was the arrival of a convoy on 14 October. The garrison saw little of the masterly seamanship by which Lord Howe manoeuvred the allied fleet out of the way. They learnt about that afterwards. What concerned them at the time was the landing of provisions, powder and shot together with two more regiments of infantry under the command of Lord Mulgrave. As from that day the Duc de

Crillon's last chance had gone. Firing continued but many of the French tents were struck on the 20th. The combined fleet under Admiral Cordova never reappeared after its brush with Lord Howe and more supply ships entered without hindrance, bringing mail for the garrison and two letters for Richard Delancey.

The one with the Admiralty seal conveyed the news that his promotion had been confirmed. The mere superscription conveyed the essential fact, reading "Richard A. Delancey, Esquire." He had officially become a lieutenant in the Royal Navy, something far above his early expectations. He was at the same time posted to the *Brilliant,* under the command of Sir Roger Curtis. The frigate had been refloated by this time but Richard had no illusions about his future. There were rumours of peace and he knew that the *Brilliant* would be paid off and that he would never be offered another berth until another war began. He was lucky to have his commission. He would not have had that after the preliminaries of peace had been signed. He would now have his half-pay but would nevertheless have his living to seek.

The other letter came from Gabriel Andros, a cousin he could barely remember, and was dated from Guernsey on 18 July 1782:

Dear Richard,

It is with the greatest regret that I have to acquaint you with the death of your mother who dyed last month of a fever. She had been ailing ever since your father's death last year and her neighbours thought that she had no great inclination to survive after the loss of two sons and after hearing the rumour, mercifully false, that you too had perished in America. As you know, she saw little of her relatives from the time of her marriage which some thought ill-

advised but several of them attended her funeral with every
sign of respect and grief. She left no will and testament but
there is no doubt that you are her only male heir standing
to inherit half of what property she left, the remainder
going to yr sister, Rachel. Her fortune was inconsiderable,
as you can well understand, but there is a summ left for
you with her advocate amounting to rather less than a hundred pounds sterling (I spare you the livres tournois which
you have most likely forgotten the value of). I have also to
inform you that I have heard from my cousin, Edmund.
You will recall that the outbreak of war came when you
were going to join his father's counting-house in Liverpool.
The trade prospects were then poor indeed for a firm deal-
ing largely in America and the Mediterranean but the
comming of peace should renew the prosperity of Messrs
Preston, Steere & Andros. It would not appear from his letter that Edmund is himself very active in the business but
he tells me of another partner, Mr Carslake, who has great
plans for the Barbarie trade. Wishing to see the family still
represented in the firm's transactions, Edmund would consider bringing you into the business as clerk or agent and
begs that you write to him at the firm's address in Dale
Street, Liverpool. I trust you will see this as an opening
which it would be foolish to ignore. I must not end this
letter without assuring you of the continued prosperity and
health of your sister, Mrs Sedley, who now resides in a verie
respectable part of Bristol where she is bringing up several
of your nephews and nieces. I remain with great truth your
sincere friend and cousin,

Gabriel Andros

Richard had not even heard of his father's death so that this letter came as a double shock. He wondered whether he had written as often as he should and whether it was for want of a letter that his mother had died. Hers had been a sad life, though, and his father's perhaps still more so except for that brief period of prosperity which had just sufficed to place his one remaining son on the quarterdeck. Their little tragedy was over now, nothing left but two nameless graves in a churchyard. As for his own career, it seemed that the closing of one door had led to the opening of another. Without deciding anything now, he would certainly write to his cousin when the time came. Why not? He knew that there were possibilities in the Barbary trade and the coast of Barbary was fairly in sight from Gibraltar itself. He could see it, indeed, from where he stood, much as Sark can be seen from St Peter Port. He might even return to Gibraltar in time of peace . . . Such possibilities would have to wait, however, for there was work to do and the gunboats were still active, rowing guard, and were sometimes even in action.

There were a few casualties in one skirmish and Richard was careful to visit the hospital afterwards. He said what he could to cheer his men up and was leaving by the main entrance when an orderly ran after him, begging him to return. The chief clerk of the hospital asked the favour of a word with him. Somewhat mystified, Richard walked back to the entrance hall where the chief clerk, Mr Garston, was waiting.

"I beg pardon, Mr Delancey," said that official, "but I am glad you chanced to call. It's about old Captain Bradshaw . . ."

"Yes, I heard that he had been killed. What a shame it was that the hospital should be accidentally hit. I suppose he might have recovered?"

"No, sir. He was dying and he knew it. That is why he told me how to dispose of his few belongings. He had drawn up a will years ago which covered his property in Hampshire. He had only his sea-chest here, with his uniform and suchlike, and he directed that all should be sold and the money given to the hospital staff who had looked after him. That has been done but the sale was not to include his sword. He said before me and two other witnesses that his sword was to go to the young man in whose examination he had assisted. We said 'Yes, yes' the way we do with men who are very ill but we had no idea what he meant. I have inquired around for weeks past and then I had the wit to ask the senior surgeon, Mr Forbes, who has been here throughout the siege. He was none too certain—he has had work enough since, as you can imagine, with all those poor Spaniards —but he remembered that Captain Curtis, Sir Roger as he is now, had asked permission to visit the old captain with two other officers. He had agreed, none too readily I should guess. He told me, however, that Sir Roger had gone back to London with despatches but that one of the other officers might still be there. This led me to Captain Gibson who told me the whole story."

"I wonder that Captain Bradshaw was well enough to make this disposition. He was far gone, it seemed, on the day when I took my examination."

"He had his ups and downs, his good days and his bad days. He was sitting up on the day he sent for me. Yes, he knew his mind that day. I think you must once have done him a kindness."

"And I suppose the sword was at his bedside and so destroyed by the shot or the falling masonry?"

"No, sir, the sword was in my office and is still there, as good as ever. If you'll wait a moment, I'll fetch it. It's not a fancy sword, mind you, not a presentation sword from the town of Plymouth. Nothing the like of that. But it's a good useful weapon and he wanted you to have it. Wait here, sir, while I fetch it."

The chief clerk was gone for a few minutes and Richard had time to look about him. The entrance hall was undamaged but looked rather bleak and shabby. There were oblong patches on the walls, showing where the pictures had hung before they were removed to a place of safety. From the north end of the building came the sound of hammering—repairs had already begun. Then Mr Garston returned, carrying the sword.

"Here it is, sir, and I brought the sword belt as well. The hilt is gold-plated, not brass, and it is little the worse for wear. I kept it wrapped up, you see, in a piece of cloth, and the blade is well greased, without so much as a spot of rust."

"Thank you, Mr Garston." Richard took the sword and examined it carefully. It had certainly been well looked after, needing only some polish and leather cream. He drew the blade far enough from the sheath to read the maker's name: Wilkinson Sword Company. He sheathed it gently again, put on the sword belt and hung the sword in position.

"Funny thing," said Mr Garston, "the old gentleman was more aware of things that day than the other officers imagined. Anyway, he remembered your examination afterwards and laughed about it. You were asked nothing, he said, about seamanship or navigation. They had decided beforehand that you were to pass."

"That I am not to know, Mr Garston. But it's quite true that I was examined in military engineering and siege warfare. Sir Roger was every inch a soldier at that time. He is a seaman again now."

"The old captain chuckled over that. He had no doubts about your seamanship, having talked with you one time, but the examination, he said, merely proved that you were a soldier. In his day, he said—begging your pardon, sir—they would have failed you for not sticking to your own trade."

"I've no doubt of it, Mr Garston, and what you say serves to remind me that I must return to duty. Thank you for all the trouble you have taken. I am proud to have this sword and will take good care of it."

Richard took his leave and strode out of the hospital, the sword at his side. He was faintly self-conscious, aware though he was that nobody in the fortress would give him a second glance. More alone in the world than ever, and totally lacking any fortune or interest, he knew himself to be a commissioned officer, a seaman and a gentleman.

NEW! The Privateersman Mysteries

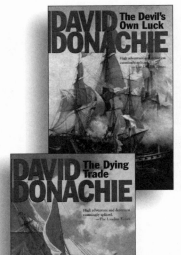

The Privateersman Mysteries, Volumes 1 & 2

"Not content to outflank and out-gun C.S. Forester with his vivid and accurate shipboard action, storm havoc and battle scenes, **Donachie has made Ludlow the most compulsively readable amateur detec- tive since Dick Francis' latest ex-jockey."** —*Cambridge Evening News*

In this exciting new series—available now for the first time ever in the U.S. in hardcover and quality trade paperback—David Donachie re-invents the nautical fiction genre with his smart, authentic, action-filled shipboard whodunits set in the 1790s during Britain's struggle with Revolutionary France.

Donachie's hero, Harry Ludlow, is an admiral's son who was raised to serve. When he is forced out of the navy under a cloud, Harry becomes a privateersman in partnership with his younger brother James, a rising artist with his own reasons for leaving London. Together, murder and intrigue take more of their time than hunting fat trading vessels.

From the dark bowels of a troubled ship of the line to the rough-and-tumble docks of Genoa, Harry is stalked by the specter of murder. In the roiling waters of the West Indies and the Spanish colony of New Orleans, he is caught up in the intrigues of great nations and the power plays of men far from the control of governments.

THE DEVIL'S OWN LUCK
ISBN 1-59013-003-0 • 6" x 9"
320 pp., $23.95 hardcover

ISBN 1-59013-004-9 • 5.5" x 8.5", 304 pp., $15.95 quality trade paperback

THE DYING TRADE
ISBN 1-59013-005-7 • 6" x 9"
400 pp., $24.95 hardcover

ISBN 1-59013-006-5 • 5.5" x 8.5", 384 pp., $16.95 quality trade paperback

"High adventure and detec- tion cunningly spliced. Battle scenes which reek of blood and brine; excitements on terra firma to match."
—*Literary Review*

Available in bookstores, or call toll-free:
1-888-BOOKS-11 (1-888-266-5711).
To order on the web: **www.mcbooks.com**
and read an excerpt.

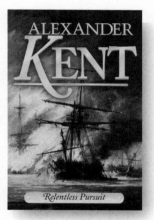